# *Cassie's Conundrum*

## A Tale of Forbidden Lust

Photo Credit: © Can Stock Photo Inc./lunamarina

ISBN-13: 978-0692720653
ISBN-10: 0692720650

Printed in the United States of America.

Forelsket Press  •  Las Vegas, Nevada

# Also by J.W. Richard

## Oral Anxiety
*A Woman's Battle with Her Sexual Demons*

## Crossed Signals
*One Couple's Journey of Sexual Discovery*

## A Cougar Falls
*Stunning Consequences*

## The Roles We Play
*A Spank-tacular Tale*

*Brothers and sisters are as close as hands and feet.*

— Vietnamese proverb

# Preview

She sat on the edge of the bed and watched the twitching of his blood-gorged muscle. Cassie looked toward him, his eyes pleading with her, his arms spread apart and raised slightly by the bindings fastened to the headboard. Jake's wrists were so loosely tied that a firm tug would set him free but she knew he wouldn't try since that would end the fun. She leaned forward and ran her fingertips over his scrotum and up the shaft of his penis until she felt the fluid oozing from the tip. He squirmed and let out a gasp as his cock jumped in anticipation when her fingers encircled him. His gaze locked on her as she slowly moved up and down and stopped again.

"Come on already, you're driving me fucking crazy."

She smiled. "I know – that's the idea."

His ass shifted as he tried to pull against her hand. "Damn it, finish me!"

She laughed and gripped him firmly for a moment while her free hand squeezed his balls and tugged down. His breathing quickened as she started stroking him. His legs quivered, his backed arched off the bed and he let out a loud grunt as a stream of semen forcefully shot out of his cock and landed on his chest with some reaching his shoulder. She kept pumping as he continued to ejaculate, a large, white pool forming on his stomach. The amount of fluid that he generated always astounded her and she never grew tired of watching him cum.

His head dropped back on his pillow, his eyes were closed and his arms relaxed. His breathing started returning to normal as his penis began to go flaccid. His eyes opened and looked at her as he tugged himself free of the bindings. She wiped her hand on his thigh to remove some of the goo that covered it. Her gaze followed the semen trail from his belly to his chest as her fingers wiped off the small glob that sat on his left shoulder.

"Almost made it," she said. "A little more teasing and I'll get you to squirt yourself in the face yet."

"You're evil," he said.

"I know, and you love it."

"Damn straight."

She shook her head and grinned as she watched a rivulet of semen trickle down his side. She forgot to bring a towel with her so she started to get up and get one when a car door slammed and she heard footsteps coming up the walk.

"Shit, mom's home!"

"Fuck, she's early."

She ran to the hall linen closet, grabbed a towel, turned and tossed it to him. "Get cleaned up – I'll stall her."

# Cassie's Conundrum

# Chapter One

## *June, 2016*

An empty plate sat on the kitchen table, the dirty one already in the dishwasher. Cassie put away the remains of another dinner prepared for two but eaten by one. Maybe it really wasn't his fault this time. She understood full well that a cop often works past the scheduled end of a shift. She just wished he hadn't called to say he was on his way; at least he could have called again to say he'd be late. She would give him the benefit of doubt – again – but her patience had worn paper thin. On top of all that she was incredibly horny.

She sat on the sofa in her robe for a while absently watching TV. She thought about masturbating but really needed a man's touch so she held off and would only do herself as a last resort. About an hour later she heard his car pull in the driveway and got up to meet him in the kitchen. Cassie was waiting as he came through the door. She took his coat, kissed him hello and smelled the beer on his breath. She bit her tongue and reheated his dinner while he changed into his sweats.

As he sat down she put his plate in front of him. "Why didn't you call to let me know you'd be late?"

"Sorry Cas, I got stuck on a fatal detail on the interstate and couldn't call."

"They have bars on the interstate now?"

He looked at her. "C'mon Cas, I needed to blow off a little steam. It was a bad one, besides I only had two."

Cassie let it go. If she harped on it any more they would just have another fight that no one wins. Instead she poured herself a glass of Chablis and returned to the couch. Ten minutes later he joined her with a beer in hand. After sitting next to her quietly for a few minutes – probably trying to gauge how pissed she was – he moved a little closer and put his leg over hers. She *was* pissed but when his leg touched her she felt a jolt of electricity run through her. *God I'm fucking horny.* As he watched TV, he slipped a hand inside her robe and felt her nipple. She closed her eyes and emitted a soft sigh. She slipped her hand inside his sweats until she reached his cock. He was at about half-mast and growing. She flung her robe open exposing herself and spreading her legs, hoping he would get the hint. Cassie rubbed his now-erect penis as he pulled his sweats down enough to fully expose himself. His fingers found her pussy and played with it but that wasn't what she wanted.

She let go of his cock. "Eat me."

He rubbed her clit. "Do me first."

She hated this game but she went along with it anyway. She slid off the couch and positioned herself in front of him. He dropped his sweats to his ankles and scooted forward to give her easy access. She lowered herself toward his cock but recoiled at the smell, he hadn't showered since that morning. She worked him with her hand for a moment and then took him in her mouth. When she wanted to please him with a blowjob she knew how to make it last and give him maximum pleasure. This was not one of those times. She pumped with her hand as she sucked and licked and made him cum as quickly as she could. She swallowed the small amount of semen he ejaculated and realized he must have cum very recently even though they hadn't done anything in over a week. *Maybe he jerked off...maybe he had some help.*

Cassie got up and went to the bathroom to give her mouth a quick rinse and get his funky taste off of her lips. Two minutes later she returned to the living room to see he'd pulled up his pants and was engrossed in the television. *Now* she was really pissed. She stood there, let her robe fall open and put her hands on her hips to hold it back. She waited for him to acknowledge her presence as she stood there with her pussy facing him and accusing him of cunnilingual neglect. He finally looked up.

Cassie tilted her head and arched her eyebrow. "What about me?"

"I'll take care of you in bed. I just want to watch this."

"Bullshit. You'll fall asleep on the couch as usual." She fastened her robe. "Why don't you just say you don't like eating me?"

"C'mon Cas..."

"Is my pussy that bad? You used to like it...or at least you pretended to."

He looked at her then turned back to the TV. "Maybe if you shaved it."

She glared at him. "Fuck you! For eighteen months I shaved it for you! How many times did you eat me? Huh? How many?"

"I ate you plenty."

Cassie fumed. "Really? *Really?* You ate me twice!"

"It was more than that."

"Bullshit! I shaved it for eighteen months and you ate me twice. Well guess what you bastard – the blowjob factory is closed. I've sucked that miniature dick of yours for the last time."

Turning and storming out of the room, Cassie went to the bedroom and slammed the door. She sat on the bed and started to shake. This was the last straw for her and the end of yet another relationship, one that was on its last legs anyway. Another four years of her life wasted. This was a repeat of every relationship she'd ever had. *I'm forty-one, will I ever learn? Why does this keep happening to me?*

# Chapter Two

Another lackluster week passed by without incident. Jake was taking a break from the dating scene and staying home on this Friday night. He'd hoped turning forty would have opened up some new doors for his love life but it was just more of the same. His career as an engineer moved along as he'd hoped but he still had no one to share it with. His marriage shortly after graduation from college lasted all of six tedious years but at least there were no kids involved. He approached thirty with high hopes but a decade went by with only a few attempts at relationships that never went anywhere.

He hit the bars quite often and sometimes hooked up with lonely women but the sense of desperation in so many of them turned him off to anything approaching a long-term relationship. So he decided to take a month off and instead he would just do what he usually did when he came home for the night alone. It was sort of like eliminating the middleman or skipping past the preliminaries. After dinner of pepperoni pizza and a couple of beers he went to his bedroom and undressed. He came back into the living room, naked, with a towel in hand, and put a DVD in the machine. He sat in his recliner and hit play. The film started with a blowjob scene and just as he grew erect the phone rang

He paused the DVD. "Hello"

"Hey Jake, it's Cassie. I thought you'd be out for the night."

"Nah, taking a break and staying home."

"Any plans for the night?"

He chuckled. "I was just going to jerk off."

Cassie paused for a moment. "You're serious aren't you? Well, don't. I'll be over in forty-five minutes."

Jake switched off the DVD and went to take a quick shower instead. He came back into the living room twenty minutes later and removed the DVD from the player. If she was coming over on a Friday night it meant she needed to talk so he set a couple of wine glasses on the coffee table and opened a bottle of wine to let it breathe. He put some crackers on a tray and put that out as well. That task complete he went to his bedroom, got out of his robe and put on a t-shirt his pajama bottoms sans underwear. Twenty minutes later she was at the door.

Jake kissed her hello. "Rough day?"

She sat on the sofa and poured herself a glass of wine. "Trouble in paradise – again." She filled his glass. "The story of my life it seems."

Jake sat and picked up his wine. "You knew this wasn't going to last much longer. Is it done?"

"Yup. Kicked his ass out, told him to have his shit out this weekend. Which means..."

He laughed. "Which means you want to crash here for a couple of days."

"Can I?"

"Do you even have to ask?"

She leaned over and kissed him on the cheek. "Thank you."

They chatted for a bit about her fight with her now ex-boyfriend sparing no detail. She went over the chronology of the relationship and then switched to

Jakes dating problems. They talked through one bottle of wine and started a second. The conversation returned to Cassie's breakup as she sought reassurance.

"I had to end it, right?"

"Of course you did," he assured her. "One, he wouldn't eat you which shows he's not right in the head. Two, he wanted you to shave which means he has no appreciation for beauty."

Cassie laughed. "I love your reasoning."

"Just using logic."

"Did you finish your um...business before I came over?"

"You told me not to. You know me, I always listen to my big sister."

She laughed. "Yeah right. Were you using a magazine?"

"DVD"

"Well put it in, we have to watch something."

Jake slipped the DVD back in the machine, sat back down next to her and pressed play. The blowjob scene started again and they watched without talking. After the cum-shot facial the scene switched to a couple fucking. Cassie slipped her legs up on the sofa and slid next to him and rested her head on his shoulder while they watched the TV. Her finger traced his clearly visible erection for a moment before reaching into his pajamas and pulling his cock out and stroking it slowly.

Without stopping she picked her head up and looked at him. "Just to be clear – you will be eating me tonight."

Jake laughed. "Unlike some people it will be my absolute pleasure."

"Trust me, the pleasure will be all mine." She laid her head back on his shoulder and stroked. "How many times have I done this? Must be hundreds."

"At least," he said. "I'll never forget that first time you caught me naked."

Cassie laughed. "That wasn't the first time."

"What? What do you mean?"

"*Well.......*"

# Chapter Three

*October, 1990*

The aroma of meatloaf filled the kitchen. Cassie set the table as her mom whipped the mashed potatoes. The gravy bubbled and the broccoli sat in the serving dish already on the table. Her mother placed the potatoes on the side and started slicing the meatloaf and placing it on their plates.

"Go fetch your brother and tell him to get out here before dinner gets cold."

"Okay mom."

She started down the hall to Jake's room, resisting the temptation to call for him. Her mother hated when she did that, probably reminded her of all the yelling her father did when he was alive. Though she missed her dad, she didn't miss the fighting over the stupidest shit. She reached her brother's room prepared to knock but saw the door was ajar and peered in and stood there as her jaw dropped open and her breath caught in her throat. He wasn't wearing any pants. She hadn't seen him naked in years and still thought of him as a little kid. He wasn't so little anymore. His penis – no longer little boy sized – dangled beneath a dark patch of hair and his testicles hung low. She quickly composed herself and stepped back so he wouldn't realized she'd seen him.

"Dinner's ready," she said toward the door.

"Be right there."

At the dinner table Jake and her mom were quite talkative but she kept quiet.

"Something bothering you, Cassandra?" her mom asked. "You haven't said a word."

"I'm fine. I just have a test in the morning," she lied.

Jake laughed. "Worried you'll only get an A instead of an A-plus?"

Cassie made an effort to be a little more vocal through the rest of dinner. Though more involved in the conversation, she kept glancing at her brother and wondering how he had grown up without her noticing. She didn't understand why she was so surprised, he was only a little more than a year younger than her. She hit puberty at twelve sprouting pubes and boobs, why wouldn't he have hit puberty by fifteen? Shit, she'd been masturbating for two years already. Then she started wondering if he played with himself. *He must.* When did he do it? She did it when she went to bed, sometimes in the morning if she woke up early. How often did he do it? She touched herself several times a week. Did he have orgasms? She didn't, though it felt good when she touched herself. How did he do it and what was it like? She had no idea but suddenly she really, really wanted to know.

She was still a virgin and never so much as touched a guy's penis, or even saw one ready for action for that matter. She only knew what she'd been told in sex-ed classes and by her friends. She knew it got erect and ejaculated sperm but that was little more than a theoretical concept to her. So she wondered. Later that night as soon as she got in bed her hand slipped inside her panties. As her fingers spread her lips she felt incredibly wet, it was never like this before. She gasped audibly when her fingers touched her clit – it felt swollen to her – she rubbed it anyway. She fingered herself harder and faster as she went along and felt a bit dizzy but didn't stop. Her breath became rapid and shallow and her thighs started to quiver.

*Argghh!*

She tried to catch her breath as sweat covered her body. *So that's what an orgasm is like. Wow!*

There was a knock on the door and her mom stuck her head in. "Are you all right?"

"Huh? Yeah, I uh...I had a bad dream."

"Okay...if *that's* what it was."

The door closed. The smirk on her mother's face said she wasn't buying it. *It's not like you never played with yourself.* She rolled on her side and thought about her brother's penis as she drifted off to sleep.

She awoke to a knock on the door; her mother was waking her up. She sat up and stretched. She got out of bed and stripped off her panties and noticed a dark spot. She held it between her fingers and it still felt damp. *Damn.* At least she knew how an orgasm felt. She wondered if it was weird because it happened as a result of seeing her own brother's penis. She wasn't going to worry about it but she *was* going to try and see him naked again.

Over the next several days she went past his room whenever he was in there hoping to catch another eyeful. Whenever he was in the shower she tried to go in the bathroom in hopes of "accidentally" seeing him but the door was always locked. After more than a week of attempting to catch a glimpse of Jake naked, Cassie finally gave up. The idea gradually faded but never completely left her thoughts. That wasn't the only area where she wasn't having any luck. She masturbated every night now, thinking about Jake, but couldn't duplicate the orgasm she had. She did, however, discover one new thing – sexual frustration.

# Chapter Four

At school she often ate lunch with her friend Teri but this time her friend suggested going out for coffee. Cassie said she couldn't afford it but Teri insisted it would be her treat. They went to a donut shop a block away from the school. Cassie hadn't been out for coffee in a long time because it represented an unnecessary expense. Since her dad died a few years before her mother struggled to make ends meet, though she always managed somehow. She ordered a coffee and eyed the donuts but only ordered one after Teri insisted.

"I'll pay you back," Cassie said.

"Don't be ridiculous, I said I would treat."

"I don't want you to spend so much."

"Don't worry about it, really," Teri said.

They sat at one of the small tables in front of the shop and chatted about school for a bit. They almost always talked about boys and this was no exception.

Sometimes they discussed sex, though her friend probably had no more experience than she did. This time there was something she wanted to know. She hesitated for a bit but before finally broaching the subject.

"You have an older brother..."

"Two of them," Teri said, "but the oldest doesn't live home anymore."

"Ever see them naked?"

Teri seemed to hesitate. "Why do you ask?"

"I saw Jake naked."

"And?"

"Nothing, I was just walking by his room and saw him naked."

"So what's the big deal?" Teri asked.

"No big deal, I just never saw him naked before."

"Oh. Well I see my brother Brian naked sometimes, he doesn't seem to care."

"Does he ever see you naked?" Cassie asked.

"What? No, never. Though, he does sometimes ask me to show him my tits. But he's joking...I think. Did Jake see you naked?"

"No"

"Why all the questions?" Teri asked. "What's going on?"

"Nothing, just curious."

Cassie changed the subject. She wasn't sure what she'd hoped to get from the conversation but it didn't seem to help her very much at all. If anything Teri seemed very uncomfortable, this was a bit unusual for her since she was generally very open and outgoing. She had a sense her friend was holding something back.

After getting back from the coffee shop Cassie went to the rest of her classes but her afterschool math club was cancelled so she headed home early. She was glad because she would have time to work on an essay for her English class that was due later that week. Her mind preoccupied with the organization of her paper, she walked into the house and headed toward her room without realizing that Jake's books were on the table, he normally came home later than her.

She walked down the hall and noticed the door to her mother's room was open – she always closed it. Her mom's car wasn't in the driveway; Cassie thought maybe she came home for lunch and forgot to close her door. Thinking nothing more of it she kept walking until she heard a noise coming from her mom's room, it was the sound of the dresser drawer closing. Without thinking, or considering her own safety, she went to the door and stood there in disbelief. Jake stood there looking at her. In shock. Naked. Holding a pair of their mom's panties. Cassie's eyes were drawn to her brother's very erect penis. Both of them were frozen in place.

Cassie regained her composure. "What the hell are you doing?"

Jakes erection and his face both deflated. "Nothing."

"Nothing? Nothing? You have some explaining to do, or you can explain it to mom."

"No – don't tell her...please."

"Go to your room."

He quickly moved past her, dropping the panties on the bed. Cassie picked them up and followed him. She couldn't help but think his naked ass was cute as she followed behind him. She walked into his room right behind him as he reached for his pants.

"Leave them." She sat on his bed.

He stood naked in front of her. "What? Why?"

"You're not getting dressed until you tell me what this is all about." She held up the panties in her closed fist.

"Come on, let me get dressed."

"What were you doing with mom's underwear? Were you going to wear them?"

"What? No...of course not."

"Then what? Look, I'm serious. You either tell me or I'll tell mom and you'll have to tell her. Your choice, tell me or tell her."

Jake hung his head and averted his eyes. "Rub myself," he mumbled.

"What?"

"I was going to rub myself with them."

"You were going to masturbate?"

He nodded. He still wouldn't look at her. He just stood there in front of her. Naked. She was taking a good look, this is what she'd been trying to see for the last two weeks and here he was, now only a foot away from her. Naked. She would look as long as she cared to. She eyed his cock but wanted to see it erect again, she was in such shock when she caught him that she hadn't really taken a good look.

"How do you do it?" she asked.

"Huh?"

"How do you masturbate?"

"I rub it."

"How often do you play with yourself?"

"Every day."

Cassie was surprised. "You do masturbate *every* day?"

"Uh huh, sometimes more than once."

"Wow," Cassie said. "Do you do it standing up? Do you lie down? Do you sit?"

"I usually lie on the bed. Sometimes standing in the shower."

Cassie stood up and moved away from the bed. "Go ahead, lie down."

"What?"

"Lie down, I want to watch you play with yourself."

Jake didn't move. "You want to *watch*?"

"Yes"

Jake sat on the bed and lay back. He was hesitant so Cassie tossed the panties on his chest, looked at him and nodded for him to get started. He spread his legs a bit and started tugging at his penis. Her eyes were glued to it as it began to grow. *Amazing.* He started to stroke, his hand sliding up and down the shaft and over the head. He gripped it firmly and started tugging so the skin moved along with his hand. *Now I know why they call it "jerking" off.*

He looked her in the eye for the first time since she caught him. "Can you show me your boobs?"

"Hell no."

Jake closed his eyes and continued jerking his cock. He started to squirm and went faster as he breathing quickened. His legs shook and his toes curled as he grunted and shot stream of semen more than a foot into the air.

"Holy shit," Cassie said. "Holy fucking shit!"

The white fluid didn't seem to stop. It was everywhere but mostly collected on his stomach and chest. Cassie was in awe. The whole thing start to finish probably didn't take more than a minute. Jake's hand was covered with his juice and there were droplets all over him and his bed. She watched as his penis shriveled up. He started to get up but she held up her hand to stop him.

"Stay there, I'll get you a towel."

She went to the hall and grabbed a towel from the bathroom, came back and tossed it to him. He wiped himself up as she sat on the edge of the bed watching him. When he was done he draped the towel over his crotch. She pulled it away and tossed it aside leaving him exposed. He made no effort to recover himself.

"That was fucking amazing, fucking amazing." She pointed to his cock. "I can't believe all that shit came out of *that*. Fucking amazing. You do this every day?"

"Just about."

"Wow!"

Jake lifted himself up on one elbow. "So you won't tell mom?"

She smiled at him. "On one condition."

"Name it," he said.

"You let me watch again."

He grinned at her. "Deal!"

# Chapter Five

Jake couldn't believe his luck the previous afternoon. One moment he was absolutely mortified from being caught yet it turned out to be the most exciting moment of his life. One of his fantasies was to be caught and have the woman who discovered him join in – he just never expected it to be his sister and she didn't actually join in.

He was curious about Cassie to a degree and tried to see her naked at times, though not with any real effort. He would just try to take a peak when he thought he might see something. If she was wearing a loose-fitting top, which she often did, he would try to look down to see her boobs. They weren't very big but he still wanted to see; still he never saw very much of them. The only time he came close to seeing her anywhere near naked was at a beach once. She wore her bikini under her jeans and when she slipped the pants off, she accidently pulled her bathing suit bottom with them which gave him the briefest glimpse of her pubic hair before she pulled them back up. He never saw anything else.

He thought it was a bit unfair that she got to see him totally naked yet wouldn't even show him her boobs. Still he wasn't about to complain. He loved how excited she got watching him and how she became even more excited when he ejaculated. He had to work on making it last longer. He always tried to cum fast so he wouldn't get caught; now he wanted to go slow so she would watch longer. Of course that's assuming she was serious about wanting to watch again. Whether she did or didn't it was all he could think about and his ever-present hard-on was back. It didn't help that Maddie sat next to him again wearing another tight-fitting shirt.

He made it through the school day though he had been tempted to jerk off into the bathroom urinal, something he'd done a couple of times before. By his last class of the day his mind was actually on the class material instead of his dick. It helped that it was a science lab that required some focus which kept his mind from wandering. When it ended he packed up and headed for home keeping his thoughts on the homework he needed to do. That was until Maddie walked past him in front of the school and said "hi." *She said hi!* His hard-on was back.

By the time he got home his erection subsided once more as he thought about his homework again. He had a ton of it tonight and needed to get right on it. He walked in the door and saw Cassie hanging up the phone. Their paths hadn't crossed since his "performance" the night before and he wasn't sure how she would react. He decided to act as if nothing had happened and just follow her cue. She turned to him and flashed a sheepish smile as she hung up the phone.

"That was mom," she said. "She's working a little late and won't be home until after six but she's bringing home pizza."

He nodded his head. "Cool."

Cassie put one hand on her hip and shook her head while she bit her lower lip in a way that she always did but he suddenly found it incredibly sexy. "Don't just stand there – go take your clothes off!"

He hesitated briefly as she stared at him. Then he hurried to his room and started to undress. He'd stepped out of his pants and was down to his briefs and t-shirt when she stood in the doorway holding a folding chair. He looked quizzically at the chair in her hand.

"Let's go," she said. "Everything off."

He pulled the shirt over his head and tossed it aside. "What's with the chair?"

"You'll see."

She moved to the side of the bed and set up the chair facing the center of the room. He slipped off his underwear and tossed them on top of the shirt. His cock was already erect and throbbing as he stood there. Cassie sat down and just looked at him. He wasn't sure what to do so he just waited for her.

"Come closer, I want to take a good look."

He moved in until he was about a foot away from her and stopped. She looked at his penis carefully moving her head and tilting it as she examined it from every angle. She had him turn to his side and then face away from her. He felt like he was under a microscope. Finally she told him to face her again. He was hoping she would touch him but her hands stayed in her lap the entire time.

"How big is it?"

"I don't know, you're looking right at it."

"You mean you never measured it?"

He felt himself blush. "Seven and a half inches."

She smiled. "It looks really big."

He felt good when she said that, it made him proud. *She liked it.* She stood up and turned the chair around to face the bed.

"Okay, down to business." Her open palm pointed to the bed.

Jake went toward the bed. He tried to "accidently" touch her with the head of his cock as he slipped by her but she moved away to avoid him. He settled in as she sat back down in the chair with her elbows on her knees and her head in her hands as she watched him. He fondled his balls for a moment before wrapping his fingers around his cock. He started slow wanting it to last but he came on the fifth stroke. It wasn't nearly as intense as the night before but he still shot a stream that reached his chest. He kept jerking until the last drops of semen emptied and then dropped his hand to his side.

"Your dick amazes me. What does it feel like when it squirts?"

"It's really intense and then I feel light-headed. When I cum it's a relief and then I feel very relaxed."

Cassie leaned forward taking a close look at his flaccid penis and the puddle of semen that surrounded it. Jake sat there without feeling at all uncomfortable and was enjoying having her eyes on him so intently.

Cassie looked up at him. "Can you make it hard again?"

"Not for a while....though I might be able to if you showed me your boobs."

"Not happening."

"Not fair. How come I have to be naked but you don't?"

Cassie smiled. "Did you like what just happened?"

"Shit yeah!"

"Then don't complain."

"I'm not. I'd just like to see you naked."

She got up and walked out of the room then paused to stick her head back in peaking around the doorjamb. "Maybe someday."

# Chapter Six

By the following week Cassie saw Jake masturbate four times. That represented every time they were home alone together and her mom was out. It excited her and she felt disappointed when they weren't able to make it happen because one or the other wasn't home or their mom was. They set some ground rules after the last time because she was getting tired of him asking to see her naked. On the one hand she wanted to show him at least a little something since she made him strip fully every time. But she felt a bit self-conscious and wasn't ready to do so just yet. So for now he had to stop asking or she would stop watching.

She did notice that she felt differently about her brother. She saw him as a man now, not a little kid. She still played her role as big sister by being somewhat dominating and staying in control. Another result of their "playtime" was that she was constantly horny. She masturbated every night now and even had a few small orgasms though nothing even close to that first one. Every morning when she woke up her hand automatically went between her legs, though she rarely had time to play with herself then. She even started sleeping without her underwear but that would change when her period started getting close.

On Wednesday she felt a very strong urge to watch Jake and even whispered something to that effect as they crossed in the hall that morning. She thought about it all day but was extremely disappointed when she came home. Her mother's car sat in the driveway. *What the hell is she doing home so early?* When Jake came in a short time after her his frustration showed on his face. She just went about her chores and did her homework until it was time for dinner.

Cassie turned to her mother as she picked at her food. "You were home early today. Did you have a doctor's appointment or something?"

"Not at all, I just took half a day off."

"Needed a break?" Jake asked.

"No," she said. "We're doing inventory all day

Saturday and I have to work. So I figured I'd take half a day today."

Jake and Cassie looked at each other. Cassie was in much better spirits all of a sudden and Jake's frustration disappeared. They finished dinner and cleared the table. When the dishes were done and put away their mom went into the living room to watch TV. Cassie went to Jakes room and found him doing his homework.

Cassie stuck her head in his door. "I hope you didn't have any plans for Saturday."

He looked up at her and grinned. "I do now."

She walked away but quickly went back. "Oh Jake..."

"Yeah?"

"Keep your hands off your dick until then," she whispered. "I want it loaded for bear."

# Chapter Seven

As soon as Cassie left his room Jake's pants were throbbing. That morning she quickly told him to be prepared for "show time" – their new codeword for their sessions – that afternoon. His cock stayed hard all day though that typified most days lately. He barely made it to the afternoon, how could he possibly make it until Saturday? He had no idea but he would try his best.

He almost came in the bed that night just from lightly rubbing the sheets. The next morning he woke up with his cock so hard it hurt. That day he tried to concentrate on anything but jacking off. He even sat far away from Maddie and her boobs, though he was happy to see she gave him a glance that seemed to say she was disappointed. When he got home that night he was proud of himself until he realized he would have to go through the same thing again the following day. It didn't help when Cassie passed him in the hall and glanced at his crotch while biting her lower lip. That look drove him crazy.

Friday was actually easier to get through than he expected. He had a number of things going on including heading to the mall with a group of friends. He got home just in time for dinner. He picked up the aroma of tomato sauce as soon as he entered the house. He ditched his things in his room and slid into his seat just as the spaghetti was served.

"So Jacob, did you behave yourself this afternoon?" his mom asked.

Taken aback by the question he quickly glanced at Cassie who was stifling a laugh.

"Of course, mom."

"Good," she said. "I hear too many stories about rowdy teenagers at the mall."

"It was just me, Tony and Karl, hardly a rowdy bunch."

Cassie put down her fork. "So what's this inventory you have to do?"

"They do it every year," she said. "I got out of it last year but not this time. I have to be there all day from eight until five. At least they bring in lunch for us so I don't have to go out."

Cassie glanced at him and bit her lip again. He was instantly hard and wondered how he could get up from the table without his mom noticing. He had another helping of spaghetti while he waited his cock to go down. By the time he finished his erection finally subsided. Cassie had already been clearing the dishes; she came up behind him and placed her hand on his shoulder as she reached across to take his plate. When she did her boob was inches from his face and she held it there for a moment longer than necessary. He was up once more. He muttered "tease" and she stuck her tongue out at him. Now he was throbbing. *I'm never going to make it.*

# Chapter Eight

Cassie awoke early for a Saturday. She came into the kitchen just as her mom was leaving and confirmed what time she would be home. She told her not to worry about dinner because she would take care of it. After her mom left she put on a pot of coffee and rummaged through the refrigerator to see what she could make for dinner that night. After she figured it out she jumped in the shower. After a quick rinse she dressed in her tight jeans and a low-cut, form-fitting top. She appraised herself in the mirror as she turned from side to side and all around. Hopefully it was enough to drive him at least a little nuts.

When she was ready she knocked on his door to wake him up. She was standing waiting for him as he opened the door.

"Let's go sleeping beauty; I've got a big day planned for you. Go shower, I'll get breakfast ready."

She heard the shower start as she took out some bacon and eggs for breakfast and set it on the counter. She started the bacon and scrambled some eggs while it cooked. The shower stopped and she heard him get out. A few minutes later, just as she started cooking the eggs, he came into the kitchen wearing his bathrobe. She placed his plate on the table but stopped him from sitting down.

Cassie held her hand out. "I'll take the robe, you won't be needing it today."

"I have to be naked all day?"

"All day."

He slipped off the robe and handed it to her. She was delighted to see he was already erect. He sat down and started to eat while she tossed the robe into his room and returned to the kitchen. She fixed her own plate and moved to the table. Before sitting down she made a show of looking at his cock and watched it grow hard again. When it was fully erect she sat down.

"So what's the 'big day' you have planned?"

"Oh a number of things," she said. "Some experiments, some challenges. I'm sure, no I'm absolutely positive, you'll like it."

"Can you give me a hint?" he asked.

"What's the most times you've cum in a day?"

"Three...no four."

"We're going to see if we can double that."

Jake shook his head. "I doubt that."

"It's okay, I like a challenge."

After clearing the dishes she was ready for the fun to start. She went to the junk drawer and took out a tape measure and set it on the counter. Then she moved two chairs away from one side of the table to create a wide aisle.

"Let's get started. Come over here."

He stood and walked toward her. She had him stand with his back to the counter. She pulled one of the chairs about six feet away from him and sat down. He looked puzzled but didn't say anything.

"Okay," she said. "See if you can squirt on me from there."

"It'll never reach."

"Try it."

He started stroking and was breathing heavy in short order. His eyes were fixed on her – just what she wanted. She placed her hands under her breasts and lifted them while her thumbs rubbed across her nipples causing them to pop right up and show nicely through the tight top. It was more than he could stand.

*Arrgghh!*

He shot with such force that it almost hit her. It was certainly farther than she expected. He leaned back against the counter trying to catch his breath. It was the most forceful ejaculation she'd seen, even stronger than the first time. Semen shot in all directions with most of it collecting on the floor directly in front of him. As he stood there panting she grabbed the tape measure from the counter and dropped to her knees. She measured from where he stood to the furthest semen droplets.

She shook her head. "Four feet, nine inches. Fucking amazing. You almost reached me."

"God, I needed to get that out."

"Well, that's one down," she said. "Seven more to go."

"Never happen."

"Five then."

"I doubt it."

"Even if there are boobs involved?"

She watched his face light up. "You'll show me?"

"Maybe, you'll have to earn it."

"How?"

"By cumming. I'm wearing six articles of clothing. Every time you squirt from here on I'll take one off."

"I just did one."

"Doesn't count. Cum five more times and you'll see my boobs, six more and I'll be naked. You've got until four this afternoon."

She smiled as she watched his cock get hard again.

"Wow, looks like you dick's on board with the plan. You have to do it in a different position each time. Go to the sofa."

He went to the living room and she followed him. He plopped down and spread his legs wide. She dropped to the floor directly in front of him because she wanted to focus on his balls. It was taking him a lot longer this time and he'd already been going at it for several minutes. She looked away from his scrotum and up at him, he was staring directly at her. She bit her lower lip and he started to moan. *I guess he likes that.* Her gaze moved back down. He started breathing heavier and squirming. She watched as his balls tightened and drew close to his body. He let out a grunt and she felt something warm hit her face.

He caught his breath. "That's one. Take off your pants."

Cassie reached down to her foot and slipped off a sock and wiped the drop of semen off her face before tossing at him. "You get a sock."

"No fair!"

"Sock, sock, top, jeans, bra, panties – in that order. How much you see is up to you – and your dick."

# Chapter Nine

Jake felt, for lack of a better word, raw. He was having a blast playing games with Cassie but had doubts of reaching his goal. The first two times were pretty easy. He rested for thirty minutes before attempt number three and it still took twenty minutes to ejaculate. She was down two socks but he wasn't sure he would get much further; it was a lot of work just to keep it up, let alone cum.

"I need a break," he told her.

He stopped and instantly went down, though not all the way. He went to the bathroom and found some lotion to use as a lube and rejoined her in the living room. He sat in the recliner with the chair back – his designated position for this round. He put some lotion in his hand and started stroking his cock again. Fortunately it popped right back up though he had no urge to cum. She moved her chair to be closer and put her feet up close to him. She had cute feet and the toenails were painted nicely.

She started moving her feet slowly. "Imagine they were wrapped around your dick."

"There's a thought," he said.

She rubbed them together. "Moving up and down until you came."

"Oh yeah..."

He was starting to feel it. She kept moving her feet slowly, rubbing them together.

"Mmm...feels good doesn't it?"

"Oh yeah."

She started moaning as she moved her feet. Then she squirmed in her chair as he stroked faster. Finally she did that thing she does biting her lip and he let loose.

*Ughh!*

This time only a few drops came out.

"Looks like it's about empty," she said.

He watched as Cassie stood up and slowly pulled her top over her head and tossed it aside. He looked at her bra and could see the tips of her nipples through it. He realized this was as close as he was going to get. He still had time but there was nothing left in the tank. He would have to settle for staring at her bra.

"I'm not going to make it," he said.

"Don't give up," she said. "There's still time. Rest for an hour and see what happens."

"Okay."

"Look at the bright side, you learned something here. You can last a long time and you can do it more than once. Shit you've already done four, that's impressive."

He waited another ninety minutes before trying again. While waiting they spent a lot of time talking and he really appreciated how much their little game brought them together. He felt much closer to her and he told her so. She told him she felt the same way but she still wasn't taking her clothes off unless he earned it. For this attempt she told him he could choose whatever position would help him cum. He told her to lie down on her bed. When she did he climbed on and straddled her hovering just above her stomach. His goal, he told her, was to ejaculate on her. She was fine with that.

He was lubed up and stroking away but only semi-hard. He kept going anyway. He looked directly into her eyes and she stared right back at him. She alternated between licking her lips and biting her tongue which helped him get fully hard but still no urge to cum. He didn't care, he just wanted to enjoy the moment as he watched her eyes move from his to his cock and back to his eyes again. After a few minutes of this she shifted a little and rested the palms of her hands on his thighs. That was all it took.

*Agghh!*

He let out one burst of semen which landed right in the middle of her bra and just above it. He leaned back, rolled over off her and collapsed on his back. He put one arm over his forehead as he caught his breath. Cassie hopped off the bed and immediately stripped off her pants and stepped out of them. She grinned from ear to ear and twirled around slowly so he could take a good look at her. The little sliver of semen was still on her chest.

She laughed. "You did it!"

"Yeah, but I'm done."

"You sure? We still have almost an hour."

"I'm sure. But I am going to use every minute of that hour to stare at you in your underwear. I never thought I'd say this to my sister but you are fucking gorgeous!"

Cassie's eyes teared up as she beamed at him. "You really mean that?"

"Every word of it."

"Well you're pretty hot yourself and you've got a really, really nice dick."

He stood up and she surprised him by jumping up and throwing her arms around his neck and hugging him close. He hugged her back and loved the way her warm skin felt against his. He wiggled his cock in against her crotch but she made no effort to move away. Finally she moved back a little with her arms still around him.

He pulled his head back slightly and looked in her eyes. "You know, I never thought the first woman I'd hold close after sex would be my own sister."

She laughed but didn't let go. "*You* had sex, I only watched."

She finally broke the embrace and stood there with her hands on her hips looking down at his penis. "Still nothing?"

"Dead as a doornail."

"Too bad, I really wanted to be naked."

# Chapter Ten

A sense of euphoria surrounded Cassie all day Sunday. Watching him and playing games the day before made her so hot that she had another orgasm that night. She came every bit as intensely as the first time but she muffled any noise by burying her face in the pillow. Jake still looked exhausted at breakfast but when she asked him how he slept he said "like a baby" as he flashed a big smile. What really lifted her spirits so high wasn't what he did, it was what he said. She kept replaying it in her head – "*you are fucking gorgeous!*"

She wasn't sure why, but that comment meant so much coming from him. She didn't think of herself as ugly by any means but she also didn't see herself as gorgeous. She knew she had a nice body but did wish she had bigger boobs. Her friend Teri had huge breasts but she was also about fifty pounds overweight. All told, Cassie saw herself as average. As for Jake she never saw him as anything other than a little kid before but now she thought he was hot.

Something else stuck with her from their day of fun – how it felt when he hugged her. She loved the feel of his body against hers. When he pushed his penis into her it took them a little further than she planned to go. She told herself all of this was okay as long as she didn't touch him or let him touch her. Though a hug was perfectly acceptable, the contact with his naked penis was not. The problem she had was that she liked it - *she liked it*. She was also conflicted about being naked in front of him. She knew she shouldn't be but the problem was she *wanted* to be. All of this added up to the first pangs of guilt about what the two of them were doing.

On Monday she decided to talk to Teri about it. Her friend seemed unusually weird when she broached the subject previously about seeing Jake naked. She assumed that was a bad day but she would still be careful. At lunch Cassie suggested they go eat outside because it was such a nice day. They sat under a tree in a quiet part of the schoolyard.

"Remember what I told you about Jake?"

"You mean seeing him naked?" Teri asked.

"It happened again."

"Yeah? I wouldn't mind seeing him naked!"

Cassie was relieved. This was much more like Teri; she must have caught her on an off day last time.

"Well this time was a bit different."

"Tell me, tell me!"

So she told her. She spared no detail and explained it exactly as it happened but stopped short of him masturbating for her. She wasn't sure if she should reveal that but what Teri said next pushed her over the edge.

"So you made him stand there naked the whole time? Wow. Then what? How did it end?"

Cassie hesitated. "I...I made him jerk off."

"No fucking way! And he did?"

"Yup"

"I would have loved to see that."

"You don't think it was weird, me having him do that in front of me?"

"Shit no, I bet he liked it."

"He did..."

Teri looked at her and tilted her head sideways. "Something tells me there's more."

"There is...I've watched him a few times since. Is there something wrong with me?"

"No!" Teri said, then she hung her head. "I...I have to tell you something."

"What?"

"Remember I told you Brian, my brother, keeps asking me to show him my tits?"

Cassie nodded and waited for her to continue.

"Well, he would always be groping me and I got tired of fighting him off. So the next time he asked I showed him. It was just a quick flash, with my bra on. I did it to shut him up but it just made it worse, he kept badgering me for more. Then he offered to pay me five bucks if I would take my shirt and bra off and let him take a good, long look. So I did and he gave me five bucks."

Cassie was surprised by the revelation but like Teri had with her, she sensed there was more. Judging by Teri's mood as she told the story she didn't think it was bad so she asked.

"I take it that wasn't the end of it," Cassie said.

"No. It was so strange. As soon as I took my shirt off he changed. He just stared at my boobs like he was in awe. It made me feel so *good*! Then we talked, actually talked like I was a human being. I sat there with no top for over an hour and wasn't at all uncomfortable."

"What did you talk about?"

"Sex mostly. He talked about how difficult it was for him because he's fat like me and has a hard time talking to girls. The whole time I could see his dick was hard but he never tried anything. I should have had him jerk off like you did!"

"When did this happen?"

"The day we had coffee," Teri said.

"So you think it's okay that I watch Jake?"

"Yeah, as long as he likes it."

"Oh, he does."

# Chapter Eleven

Jake read the note his mother left on the kitchen table, looked at the clock and turned the oven on. He dumped his books in his room and returned to the kitchen to take the tray of chicken out of the refrigerator and place it on the counter. He took a can of soda out of the fridge and drank from it as he waited for the oven to heat up. It was another good day, they were all good lately. In the morning he felt like he'd finally recovered from Saturday. A glimpse of Maddie's cleavage and the resulting hard-on confirmed it.

He also felt good about the loan his mom gave him. Cassie's birthday was in a few days and he wanted to buy her something nice. He even set his alarm to get up before his sister so he could catch his mom alone.

"Mom?"

"Hi Jacob, you're up early."

"I need to ask a favor."

"What is it sweetie?"

"I need to borrow twenty bucks. I can work it off, do things around the house, whatever you need."

"What do you need it for?"

"It's Cassie's birthday and...and I want to buy her something nice."

"I can get her something for you."

"No. I want to get it myself. Please?"

His mother's eyes welled up. "That is so sweet of you, of course. And don't worry about paying me back, you do plenty around here."

Step one was out of the way. The tough part was that he had no idea what to get her. The dilemma did give him an opportunity to do something he'd been too chicken to do before – talk to Maddie. His heart was pounding as he walked up to her before class that day. She just sat down so he sat in his and turned to her.

"Maddie? Can I get you help with something?"

She turned to him with a curious look. "What is it?"

"You know my sister Cassie?"

"I know who she is, what's up?"

"Well, her birthday is coming up and I want to buy her something nice but I don't know what."

Maddie smiled at him. She was wearing a button-down blouse and as she leaned in toward him it billowed open and he got an eyeful of cleavage that gave him an instant hard-on. *She had to know what she was doing.*

"What's the budget?"

"Twenty bucks."

"It's getting cooler out, how about a nice sweater. See Lizzie over there? The one she's wearing would look great on your sister."

He looked at Lizzie and realized it would be perfect. "Thanks Maddie!"

"No problem, I wish my brother was like you. He lets my mother buy his gifts for him."

Step two solved, now he just had to find a ride to the mall.

The beeping of the oven signaled it was ready so Jake slid the chicken and set the timer. He placed the pots on the stove for the side dishes and, though it was normally his sister's job, he set the table. He just finished when Cassie walked in the door. He smiled at her and her face lit up.

"Someone's in a really good mood today," he said.

"It was a great day. How about you? Have you recovered?"

"Let's say I had a very 'hard' one today."

"When's mom coming home?"

He looked at the clock. "Fifty-five minutes."

She grinned. "Perfect – show time!"

"I was hoping you'd say that!"

He practically sprinted to his bedroom and started stripping off his clothes. She was right behind him and watched as he dropped on to the bed and grabbed his cock.

"Not so fast," she said. "I want to look at you."

He sat there while she looked him over. His hand moved away from his penis as he watched her eyes moving around his body.

"Do you like being looked at?

"I like it when you do it because you seem to enjoy it so much."

"Oh I do. Go ahead."

He grabbed his cock and stroked while he looked directly into her eyes. It felt good but there was no instant urge to ejaculate. He varied the speed and pressure of his strokes and could feel it starting to build. As he started going faster Cassie shifted and leaned in. Then she bit her lip.

*Arrgghh!*

# Chapter Twelve

Tuesday morning Cassie woke up before her mother's daily knock and walked into the kitchen just as her mom took her lunch bag out of the refrigerator. Cassie poured herself a cup of coffee and sat down and thumbed through the newspaper. Her mother left the room and came back a couple of minutes later holding her jacket and stood next to Cassie as she put it on.

"I'm glad you're up early," her mom said. "I wanted to talk to you."

Cassie picked her head up and looked at her. "About what?"

"About what's going on between you and your brother."

The blood drained from Cassie's face and her legs started to quiver as a chill coursed through her body. *Holy shit! How did she find out? Fuck, fuck, fuck!* She took a deep breath and did her best to compose herself.

"What...what do you mean?"

"You've changed, both of you have."

Cassie relaxed a little. "How so?"

"I'm not totally sure, but I think it's the way you treat him."

"I've always been good to him."

"That's not what I mean...it's like you started treating him like an adult all of a sudden."

Cassie felt totally relived now. "I guess I just realized he's not a little kid any more – he's...he's a man."

"Well he's certainly responded; it's like you two have suddenly grown so close."

Cassie smiled. "I think we have."

"Well I'm really happy about it," her mom said. "Whatever you're doing, keep it up."

Cassie bit her tongue. *Oh, I will!*

She saw Teri at lunch for the first time in days. She picked a table and waited for her friend to sit down with her tray. When she did she was surprised by what she had – tuna sandwich, salad and container of skim milk instead of the fried grease item of the day, bag of potato chips and can of soda.

Cassie nodded toward the food. "That's different."

"I'm tired of eating crap and feeling like shit."

"What brought this on?" Cassie asked.

"Talking with Brian."

"When you, um..."

Teri nodded. "The way he looked at me, well I want guys to look at me like that. They never will the way I look."

Cassie softened her voice. "There's nothing wrong with the way..."

"I call 'bullshit' on that. My mom's three hundred pounds and that's where I'm headed unless I do something. The problem is that my mom only buys crap and never makes a decent meal. When I ask her to buy better food she says it's too expensive but she always manages to load up on the junk food."

Cassie smiled at her. "I'm really proud of you."

"I've already lost five pounds but I'll never be skinny like you."

"And I'll never have boobs like you."

"You'd keel over if you did, you need a fat ass like mine for ballast."

They both started laughing until they were wiping tears from their eyes. Cassie was finished with her lunch and Teri suggested they head outside. When they went through the door Cassie shivered, the warm weather was probably gone until spring. They walked to a quiet spot and sat on a low, brick retaining wall and faced the school entrance. She sensed that Teri wanted to talk about something  privately so she didn't complain about the cold.

"So your little talk with your brother prompted you to diet?"

"Not a diet, a lifestyle change. And from here on it will be referred to as a 'tittie talk,' not a little talk. Besides my tits are anything but little." Teri laughed at her own comment.

"We can call it the 'tittie talk diet' – it'll be a new fad!"

"Call it what you want but I have a goal. I don't need to be skinny but I want to lose enough weight that I'm not ashamed of my body anymore. When I do I'm going to a nude beach and parade around naked for everyone to see. You can come as my witness."

"Can I keep my clothes on?"

"Sure – prude!"

Cassie laughed. "I can't believe taking your shirt off had such an impact."

"You have no idea. I feel so liberated. I was always so concerned that someone – my brother – would see me naked and always made sure it didn't happen. Now that he's seen me it doesn't matter anymore and all the anxiety is gone. It helped that he looked at me the way he did. If he'd been grossed out I would have been mortified."

"Would you let him see you again if he asked?"

Teri grinned. "Already have, only he didn't have to ask."

Cassie shifted and turned toward he friend. "Tell me, tell me!"

"I thought you'd never ask," Teri said with a chuckle. "On Saturday night when dad was out bowling and mom was at bingo I walked into Brian's room and sat down on the bed while he was playing a video game.

I do this sometimes so he thought nothing of it. As he was playing I pulled my shirt over my head and tossed it toward the doorway, I had already taken my bra off before I went in. I thought he was going to die when he turned to look at me."

"You're hot shit," Cassie said.

"He turned that game off quick. I told him it was time for another 'tittie talk' because I liked the first one so much."

"And did you..."

"After a little while I told him I wanted to see his dick. He was really embarrassed but he showed me. I never saw one before but I was surprised, I expected it to be bigger."

"Then what? What happened next?"

Teri shook her head. "He asked if he could see my cunt....my *cunt!*"

"*Eeww*, I hate that word."

"I know, me too. I told him he'll never see it if that's what he calls it. I didn't ask him to masturbate because he seemed so embarrassed. So we just sat there and talked, me with no shirt and him with his pants down around his ankles. Next time I'll ask him to jerk off."

"So that was it?"

Teri smiled. "Until next time."

# Chapter Thirteen

Jake finally made it to the mall on Wednesday after school. He couldn't get a ride so he took a school bus to a stop that was an easy walk away. He wasn't sure which store would have the best selection of sweaters so he asked Maddie. It gave him another excuse to talk to her and he was finding it easier to do so because of how she responded. After spending a few minutes chatting with her, and getting her recommendation, he had the usual hard-on. Then he realized that he hadn't cum since Monday, a longer gap than normal but not an unusually long time. It was the next realization that surprised him. Every time he'd ejaculated in the past few weeks Cassie was watching.

He made his way to the mall and found the store Maddie suggested and went in. They had quite a few really nice sweaters that were well over his budget so he kept looking in some of the other stores. He didn't find anything he liked in his price range so he went back to the first store and looked again. He finally found one that he thought was perfect but it was $24.99. He had the twenty his mom gave him and a couple dollars of his own but he was still short. Twenty was his absolute limit with his few dollars covering the sales tax. He put the sweater back and kept looking.

A cute sales clerk not much older than he was approached him. "Can I help you find something?"

He was grateful for the help. "I was looking for a sweater like this one," he pointed to the one he just put back. "But I need it to be a little cheaper."

She looked at the price tag. "How much cheaper?"

"No more than twenty before tax."

"Present for your girlfriend?"

"My sister, it's her birthday."

She put her hand on his arm. "That's so sweet." She glanced around the room and whispered, "Come with me, I'll give you my employee discount, that's twenty percent off. But you can't tell anyone."

"I won't."

She rang up his purchase, bagged it and handed it to him. "I'm Debbie, be sure to come back."

He was ecstatic about the purchase and happier still when he realized Debbie was flirting with him. Even better – he had just enough money left for the bus so he wouldn't have to walk the four miles to get home.

The bus dropped him about a quarter mile from his house. His biggest fear now was that Cassie would spot him with the package. Not only did he make it without being seen, he was relieved to see that Cassie hadn't come home yet. He took the bag into his room then went to find a box, wrapping paper, scissors and tape. He quickly realized how difficult it was to wrap a package when you'd never done it before. After four attempts he got it to a point of being almost acceptable and stashed the present under his bed. He couldn't wait to give it to her.

He didn't see her that night because she came home fairly late but he did see her the next morning. She bounced around the kitchen, obviously in a very good mood. He pretended not to know it was her birthday at first but she just stood there waiting for him to say something.

He smiled at her. "Happy birthday!"

"Don't I get a birthday hug?"

He went over and put his arms around her as she threw hers around his neck and squeezed.

"Happy birthday, sis."

"Thank you." She kissed him quickly and softly on the lips.

As she was pulling away she looked at him while biting her lower lip and winking. He was instantly hard and knew he would be all day. That was also the first time she'd ever kissed him on the lips. They separated and moved away from each other just as their mom walked in.

"Happy birthday, Cassandra! I can't believe my baby girl is growing up so fast."

"Thanks mom."

"If you guys are ready I'll drive you to school today."

In class he told Maddie about his adventure buying the sweater – sans Debbie flirting with him. She told him she was happy she was able to help and repeated how nice she thought he was for thinking of his sister. The rest of the day crawled by. He hoped Cassie would get home early but she came in just minutes before his mom. His mother walked in with Chinese food for dinner and set it on the table. After they ate his mom produced a cake with candles, from where he didn't know, and they sang "Happy Birthday" with Cassie blowing out the candles. They moved into the living room where his mom handed Cassie a well-wrapped box. She opened it to find a new pair of denim jeans. While she was hugging their mom to thank her Jake ran to his room and retrieved his present.

He handed it to her. "Sorry about the wrapping."

"You got me a present?"

Cassie tore off the wrapping and opened the box. Her mouth hung open as she held up the cream-colored, turtle neck sweater. She looked toward their mom who shook her head no.

"It's beautiful!" She started to cry.

Cassie jumped up, gave him a quick hug and sprinted to her room. She came back a moment later wearing the sweater. She twirled around for them to see.

"I love it! It's perfect. Mom, did you..."

"I had absolutely nothing to do with it."

"Oh Jake, thank you!" She hugged him and kissed him again – on the cheek this time.

When their mom left the room briefly to throw away the wrapping paper Cassie glanced at him and mouthed a silent thank you. Then she bit her lip and winked at him. In bed that night stroked himself slowly until he ejaculated. She wasn't watching but he was thinking about her.

# Chapter Fourteen

Friday morning Cassie pranced around school in her new jeans and sweater and received a number of compliments on the latter. She proudly stated to anyone who asked that her brother gave it to her for her birthday. She spoke to her mother again before leaving the house and confirmed that Jake had done it all on his own without her help. She wanted to show her appreciation but didn't know exactly how. She had some ideas but she didn't want to cross the boundaries she had set for herself regarding their "play." The primary rule being that they wouldn't have actual sex, though she was willing to go a little further than they had to this point. Not only was she willing to, she wanted to. She felt such a jolt of sexual energy when she kissed him but wasn't sure about how far to take things.

She bumped into Teri in the hall and she immediately commented on the new sweater. She told her the story and that she needed to see her at lunch. They sat at their usual table and Cassie happily saw that her friend stuck to her diet and had only a large salad on her tray. After they finished they moved outside again. The cooler air made Cassie very thankful she chose to wear the sweater.

"It's so sweet of him to buy you that," Teri said.

"I know, and I want to do something special for him...if you know what I mean."

Teri flashed a sly grin. "What were you thinking?"

"I'm not sure, I don't want to go too far. I thought about making out with him but does a guy really want to kiss his sister?"

"I don't know, maybe he does. You could ask him."

Cassie shook her head. "He wants to see my boobs but I don't think I'm ready to do that yet."

"I'll show him mine."

"That would be unfair competition – I can't compete with those jugs. Speaking of which, any new 'tittie talks'?"

"No, we haven't been alone. But..."

"What?"

"Well, something weird happened last night."
Teri hesitated for a moment before she continued. "Mom
and dad went to bed really early – I think they were
fucking. I was on the floor watching TV and must have
fallen asleep."

"It's weird that they were fucking?" Cassie asked.

"No, they do that sometimes and they aren't
exactly quiet. Though I don't know how they manage
since they're both so big."

"So what was so weird then?"

"Well, Brian was on the couch but he must have
dropped down to the floor. I was on my side and he
came up behind me. Like I said, I was sort of dozing but
not quite asleep. He snuggled in like he was spooning
but his hands didn't touch me."

"And?"

"He pushed his crotch into my ass. It woke me up
but I pretended I was sleeping. He rocked a little
pushing himself into me very gently. After doing this for
a couple of minutes he made a little noise, pushed

himself in a little harder and stopped. A minute or so later he got up and left."

"Shit"

"I think he did it in his pants."

"Did you say anything?"

"No"

"Why not?"

"I kind of liked it. I might bring it up at our next talk but I don't know. I'll see how he is."

Lunch time ended and they hurried to get back to class. As she thought about Teri's story, the germ of an idea popped into her head. Cassie worked through the logistics the idea took shape as she walked down the hall. By the time she reached her class she knew what she was going to do and smiled broadly. *Fuck yeah!*

# Chapter Fifteen

Jake lathered up in the shower and used the scented body wash Cassie gave him because she liked the way it smelled. All day long his mind had been fixated on one thing – releasing the load that drove him crazy since ten that morning. Maddie "big boobs" started it, as usual, by wearing a tight t-shirt and thin bra and sitting next to him. He stared at her all through history class and at one point he realized he could see the outline of her nipples – or at least he imagined he could. About halfway through class he almost came in his pants when her nipples hardened briefly as he watched. Maybe she knew he was looking and by now she probably figured out that she drove him absolutely crazy. Whatever the case, his hard-on was with him the entire day.

When he arrived home Cassie was already there in her room and his mom wasn't home, exactly as he hoped. He quickly ditched his books, stripped and jumped in the shower. A month ago he would have jacked off as soon as he got home, now he hoped for more and was rarely disappointed. He rinsed the soap off his body making sure his cock and balls were clean. Stepping out of the shower he dried himself while gazing in the mirror looking at his erection. *Damn thing is never satisfied.* His hand circled his cock and squeezed giving him an immediate urge to ejaculate. He hated that he didn't last very long but it was getting much better, the good thing was Cassie didn't seem to mind.

Jake wrapped the towel around his waist just in case his mom came home unexpectedly. He left the bathroom and went to the kitchen to be sure the coast was clear and looked out the window to be sure her car wasn't there. She wasn't due home for two hours but he wanted to be certain. He walked back down the hallway hoping Cassie's door wasn't closed since it was her firm rule that he wasn't allowed to disturb her if it was. He walked toward her room, his cock straining against the towel. The door was ajar. *Yes!* He stopped and peaked in and almost came on the spot. She was facedown, resting on her elbows reading a magazine. One leg bent up at the knee with her foot twitching slowly. She was only wearing a bra – no underwear – her ass was bare! Two pale-white was gorgeous cheeks beckoned.

In the past several weeks he jerked off in front of her fourteen times, he was counting, but he'd never seen her nude. The closest he came happened that Saturday when she was in her underwear. He tried to get her to at least show him her boobs one more time since then but she refused and said if he pushed again she wouldn't watch him anymore. So he didn't push. Now as he stared at her he didn't know what to do so he just stood there.

She turned her head toward him without changing position and grinned. "Don't just stand there; close the door. And get rid of the fucking towel."

He let the towel fall to the floor as he turned and shut the door. When he spun around toward her she'd turned back to her magazine. He wasn't sure what to do. Should he touch her? Touch himself? He didn't know so he just stood there. A moment later she looked back at him and started to laugh.

"Don't just stand there."

"Wha...what do you want me to do?"

She bit her lower lip as she looked at his cock. "Rub your dick on my ass."

"You want..."

"Stick your dick between my cheeks and rub."

He tentatively climbed on her bed and straddled her. She slipped a pillow under her to raise her ass a bit. He slid down and nestled his cock between her cheeks and started moving back and forth. He couldn't believe how good it felt, his cock never touched bare skin other than his own before and her ass was so soft and warm. Though he'd built up enough stamina to last several minutes when masturbating, this only took a few strokes.

*Argghh!*

His semen shot a line up her spine to just above her bra strap. He rocked against her as he kept ejaculating forming a white puddle in the small of her back. He was light-headed for a moment but slowly caught his breath. He never felt anything remotely like that before.

# Chapter Sixteen

The hot fluid landed on her spine an instant after his loud grunt. She felt Jake's legs quivering as they pressed against her thighs while he continued sliding his cock against her ass. His semen now landed in the small of her back and pooled up. She felt it oozing as he stopped moving and slowly regained his composure. He climbed off of her. She went back to her magazine as he retrieved the towel and wiped his juice off of her back. When he was done she pulled the sheet over herself and turned on her side.

She patted the bed. "Sit down."

He sat on the bed next to her with one leg on the floor and the other bent at the knee, resting on the bed. The towel covered his lap. She grabbed it and tossed it aside leaving him exposed, his penis shriveled with a small glob of semen on the tip.

"You know better than that. How am I supposed to look at your dick if you cover it up?"

"Sorry, it's a reflex."

She looked him in the eyes and grinned. "How was that?"

"Un-fucking-believable. I never felt anything like that, your ass is so soft and...and...it's fucking gorgeous."

His comment gave her goose bumps. She soaked in the compliment as her gaze returned to his cock. She loved the way it felt – the way he felt – as he rubbed it on her. She resisted the urge to reach out and hold it. She wanted to take it in her hand and feel it, watch it grow, feel him as he came. She thought about that a lot lately but couldn't get past the idea that brother and sister didn't do that. She looked away from his penis and up at him. He'd been watching her look at him.

"I enjoyed it too," she said. "I guess it's safe to say that was your favorite thing we've done."

"Second favorite."

"Second? What was first?"

He stared into her eyes for a moment before he answered. "When you kissed me."

Her mouth fell open and her eyes filled with tears, something that seemed to happen a lot lately. She sat up and her hands reached for his head, grabbed it and pulled him close. She brought her lips to his and kissed him softly, pulled away, kissed him again and felt him respond. She pulled away one more time, looked him in the eyes and moved back in with her mouth open. He tongue pushed his lips apart and found his tongue as they explored each other, her into his mouth then him into hers. She felt the wetness in her vagina as it started tingling, electricity coursed from her lips to her nipples and down to her clit. When she pulled away a few minutes later she was totally out of breath, as was he. His cock stood erect and throbbing once more.

Cassie flipped on her stomach and tossed the sheet aside. "Do it again, nice and slow."

He stepped off the bed and moved to the side. She felt him climb back on and straddle her once more. His hand gently touched her ass and moved up and down caressing each cheek causing her to inhale sharply. She turned her head around and saw him just looking and admiring her ass as he rubbed it so tenderly. She turned her head back around and brought herself to the pillow as he lowered himself onto her. One hand spread her cheeks as he place his cock between them, released his hand and started to rub up and down her butt crack. She closed her eyes and concentrated on how his cock felt as he moved.

This went on for three or four minutes until he started breathing heavier and moving faster. He pushed himself into her ass with a little more force and moved rapidly before grunting and collapsing on top of her. His weight settled on her as he moved to finish ejaculating. He pushed himself up with his hands to take his weight off of her.

"No, no – lay on top of me like you were."

He settled back down, turning his head to the side and settling into her left shoulder. Her right hand found his and she interlaced her fingers with his. Her left hand reached up and found his head as she ran her fingers through his hair. She murmured with contentment. She felt – *safe*.

# Chapter Seventeen

Jake went to school Monday still thinking of Friday afternoon. All weekend long he kept replaying it in his mind and he and Cassie cast sly glances and knowing looks at each other ever since. They couldn't talk about it because they were never alone. The picture of her ass inked indelibly in his mind, he looked at other girls and tried to imagine if derrières looked anywhere near as nice. One thing for sure, he couldn't wait to see it again.

He walked into class right behind Maddie and rather than eyeing her boobs his gaze went to her ass. Much bigger than his sister's but still well-proportioned, he wondered if it could possibly be as soft. She sat in her seat and he slid into the one next to her. While taking his notebook out of his backpack he heard a voice talking to him and realized it was Maddie.

"I saw your sister Friday afternoon," Maddie said. "She was wearing a sweater, was that the one you bought her?"

His throat suddenly went dry. "Yeah"

"Well you did a great job picking it out, it looked great on her."

His lips felt parched now as well. "Thanks."

"Um...are you going to the sophomore social on Friday?"

"I wasn't planning on it," he said.

He suddenly realized his mistake. She – *Maddie* – was asking him out. And he just screwed it up. *What an ignoramus!*

"Oh, I was hoping you'd be there."

He seized his chance at redemption. "Then I'm definitely going."

Her face lit up. He could almost swear that her nipples got hard – he knew his dick sure did.


Jake ate lunch with his buddies Karl and Tony as he did most days. He wanted to tell them what happened that morning but didn't want to make a big deal about it in case Maddie wasn't really asking him on a date. The more he thought about it the greater his feeling that he would just be part of a large group. Whatever the case, he was just excited for the opportunity to see her outside of class and that she cared enough to ask him.

"Hey Jake," Karl said, "We're going to the mall after school Friday so tell your mom you'll be home late."

"Um, I can't."

"What do you mean you can't?"

Tony laughed. "He probably has to help his sister with something again."

"Hey, I wouldn't mind 'helping' his sister with a few things myself," Karl said.

Jake realized he'd been avoiding his friends and using Cassie as an excuse. He wanted to be home every day so he wouldn't miss out on opportunity with Cassie. If his friends noticed it meant he had to be more careful and maybe dial things back a bit. The problem was that he had absolutely no desire to.

"It has nothing to do with my sister. I'm going to the sophomore social after school."

Tony laughed again. "Really? That's for nerds and geeks, why would you go to that?"

"Because I'm going with Maddie."

"Maddie?" Karl said. "No fucking way!"

"Tits McGee?" Tony said. "Get the fuck out! You had the balls to ask *her* out?"

Jake smirked. "She asked me."

"What? No way, no fucking way."

"Get the fuck out! Maddie big tits asked you out? *You?* No fucking way!"

# Chapter Eighteen

Cassie looked for Teri all day Monday but never saw her. She needed to talk to someone about Friday and her friend was to only one she could possibly share this with. She couldn't shake the idea that she'd gone too far but, despite the pangs of guilt, she loved every minute of it. She had an urge to touch Jake's cock that bordered on uncontrollable. The feel of his body on hers, the feel of his cock, his weight on her, his semen when he ejaculated on her were driving her insane. In a way she was glad that her mom was home all weekend or she definitely would have gone for it.

On Tuesday Cassie finally saw Teri and told her to meet her at lunch. She arrived at the cafeteria to find Teri already eating. She didn't bother getting in line for food and went straight to the table instead and sat down, happy to see Teri was sticking to her diet."

"Not hungry today?"

"I'll grab something later," Cassie said. "I missed you yesterday.

"Bad cramps so I stayed home."

"Mine's due any day," Cassie said. "I don't get why they call it your 'friend' – periods suck."

"It does put a damper on things."

"Speaking of things, how's the diet?"

"Lifestyle change and I'm down eight pounds."

"It's starting to show," Cassie said.

Teri beamed. "Really? I've been afraid I'll lose it all in the boobs. They say that's the last place you gain and first place you lose. I really want to lose it from my ass, though that's been pretty useful lately."

Cassie cocked her head to the side. "How so?"

Teri finished her lunch."Let's go outside."

They went out to their usual spot. It was only a little chilly but Cassie still zipped up her jacket.

"So what's your ass up to now?"

Teri laughed. "Remember when I told about...

"When you fell asleep?"

"Uh huh. Well we had a 'tittie talk' and I brought it up. He tried to act like he didn't know what I was talking about. So I stood in front of him about a foot away, held up my boobs and said 'confess to the titties'."

"And?"

"He admitted it. He said he couldn't help himself and he apologized. He said it wouldn't happen again and I told him that was too bad because I liked it. You know the expression 'didn't know whether to shit or get off the pot?' Well, that was Brian."

Cassie laughed at the image. "Then what? Don't tell me that was it."

"Hell no. I told him to stand up and drop his pants and he did. I walked over to his dresser and leaned on it bending forward a bit. I pulled my sweats down just enough to expose my butt without letting him see my bush and told him to rub his dick against me."

"He didn't cum on the spot? Jake would have."

"It takes him a while. He shot when I let him feel my boobs."

"I let Jake see my ass," Cassie said.

She'd intended to tell Teri everything but something made her hold back. The conflict between doing what she knew was right and doing what she really wanted to do kept gnawing at her. One moment she convinced herself she needed to back off and the next she couldn't wait to feel him on her again. She also knew that the next time she got the urge to grab his cock she wouldn't be able to stop herself.

"So you showed him your ass but still no boobs?"

Cassie shook her head. "No boobs."

"Offer stands, I'll show him mine. I think I'm turning into an exhibitionist."

Cassie laughed. "You're too much. Do you ever get the urge to feel Brian's dick?"

"Yeah"

"Me too, and its driving me nuts. I know I shouldn't be doing this."

"Why not?"

"Because it's wrong," Cassie said.

"According to who? Our fucked up society? I don't see anything wrong with it as long as no one's being hurt. You both like it, Brian and I like it. As long as it's fun do it."

"I guess you're right."

They left to go to class. Cassie needed to make a

decision. She either had to do it without guilt or stop completely. Her mind tossed it around all afternoon. If she didn't stop completely she had to go further or she would drive herself crazy. The sudden cramp in her abdomen told her she wouldn't need to worry about for a few days. After class she went to the ladies room and inserted a pad in case she started flowing before she got home. When she came out of the bathroom Derek was waiting for her. He'd asked her out several times but she always made excuses to turn him down. He wasn't a bad guy and other girls thought he was hot because he played football. That didn't do anything for her and she wasn't really attracted to him but she did kind of like him.

"Hi Cassie."

He seemed really nervous and she thought that was cute. Maybe going on a date would help settle her mind about her brother. She looked at him closely. Not bad looking, a few pimples but not too many, certainly had muscles if you liked that sort of thing and he didn't act *too* much like a jock.

"What's up Derek."

"I um...I was wondering if you might like to see a movie on Saturday, maybe grab a bite too."

She stood there silently for a moment taking in his nervousness and letting him fidget while he waited for an answer. "I'd love to."

"Really? Great! I... um... I can pick you up, I'll have my mom's car. Is seven okay?"

"That's fine."

"Great, see you then." He started walking away before turning back quickly. "I, um, don't know where you live."

She laughed and wrote down her address and phone number and handed it to him. He took it and thanked her before turning away again. *Hope you didn't shit your pants.*

# Chapter Nineteen

By Wednesday Cassie was flowing heavy and experiencing intermittently bad cramps. She made it through school but came home and curled up on the couch in her sweats and sat in front of the TV. The first two days were the worst which meant she should be fine for her date on Saturday. Jake came home and when he caught sight of her he surely had to figure out there would be no show time today. He walked in to the living room and his look of concern touched her.

"Are you sick?"

"Moon time."

"Huh?"

"I have my period."

"Oh. Can I do anything?"

A cramp hit her and she scrunched up her face. "You're sweet, but no."

She closed her eyes and tried to doze. She heard him banging things around in the kitchen and wished the noise would stop. It quieted down for a few minutes then things started clinking again. *What is he doing in there?*

He came back into the living room and handed her a cup. "I made you some tea."

She sat up and took the cup from him. Her eyes filled up with tears and she almost started to cry – moon time is emotional time.

"Thank you, that was so nice of you."

He started walking away. "You're welcome. I thought it would make you feel better."

She smiled at him. "Come sit with me for a few minutes."

He sat across from her as she sipped her tea. She was touched by how concerned he looked and felt a need to reassure him she was okay.

"I'm not dying, I go through this every month. How was your day? Anything exciting going on?"

"Same as always," he said. "I am going out on Friday."

"The mall with your hooligan friends?"

"The sophomore social."

"Really? What made you want to go to that?"

"Maddie invited me."

"Maddie?"

"Maddie McGee, you probably don't know her."

"No I guess...wait a minute. Not *that* Maddie....the one with the..."

"That's the one."

"She's a pair of boobs with feet. The girls are always talking about her – it's not fair that a sophomore should look like that. You asked *her* out?"

"She asked me."

Cassie smiled at her brother. One of the hottest girls in the school asked him out. Then she had a strange feeling in her gut and it wasn't a cramp, it was a pang of jealousy.

# Chapter Twenty

Friday started at warp speed then seemed to crawl for Jake. His morning class with Maddie went by too fast and her comment about seeing him later ratcheted his excitement level up more than he thought possible. What she wore kicked things up another notch entirely. Quite often she dressed in loose-fitting tops that downplayed her figure, as if that were remotely possible, but not today. She dressed to kill and he couldn't wait for the social. Once that class ended he watched the clock constantly causing minutes to seem like hours. The school hosted a number of events throughout the year designed to bring students together, this would be the first one he ever attended. He thought along the same lines as Tony and Karl believing that they were for kids that didn't really fit in. If Maddie wanted to attend it couldn't be that bad since she was hardly a misfit and easily stood among the most popular kids in school.

At lunch he put up with a lot of ribbing from his friends. *Have fun with mammary Maddie, remember it takes two hands to handle her whoppers, give her bazongas a squeeze for me.* He laughed along with them and didn't really mind because he knew they were jealous. He was surprised, though, by Cassie's reaction, she didn't seem to like Maddie for some reason. He didn't think that was fair since his sister didn't even know her. He got the impression that Cassie, like a lot of other girls, was jealous of Maddie's breasts. Jake freely admitted that the boobs are what attracted him to Maddie in the first place, but he liked her because of the way she talked to him.

The social started at four that afternoon and was held in the school gymnasium. Small, high tables were set up without chairs. The idea was to prevent people from sitting in one spot so they would move about and mingle. He wanted to meet up with Maddie well before hand and walk in with her but she nixed that suggestion and told him just to arrive a few minutes early. When he walked in at the appointed time she was already there standing at a table and surrounded by half a dozen guys – exactly what he was afraid of. His heart sank. He headed in her direction and his spirits were lifted a little when she spotted him and waved him over.

He reached the table and she made room for him to stand next to her. He stood there while the guys vied for her attention and, at least he thought, made stupid comments to try and impress her. She listened politely for a few minutes before deftly excusing herself and pulling him away. He was impressed by how smoothly she extricated herself, probably the result of a lot of practice. He followed her to a table surrounded by a few girls. Maddie said hello to them but they seemed somewhat cool to her. After a few minutes they moved again.

For an hour they drifted from table to table but wherever they went guys followed. The entire time he barely got a chance to talk to her and, though he liked being near her, he felt like he made a mistake in coming. Some guys would try talking while others just looked at her. One guy stared so intently at her chest with his mouth hanging open that he seemed oblivious to everything else. Jake glared at him until he looked up and saw his gaze and slinked away red-faced. Maddie caught sight of the silent exchange and realized what happened. She hooked her arm in his, excused herself and pulled him away.

"Thank you."

He mumbled something but didn't really know how to respond. She led him to the side of the gym near an exit door. She glanced to be sure a chaperone wasn't watching and slipped outside pulling him along by the hand. Their jackets were inside but it wasn't too cold yet since the sun hadn't gone down. He followed her to a set of steps near a different entrance and sat down next to her. She leaned into him just a little so their arms touched. The chill he felt had nothing to do with the weather.

"I appreciate what you did in there."

"I didn't do anything," he said.

She ignored his comment. "That happens all the time as you can imagine. That's why I sometimes dress in loose clothes."

He found this to be a contradiction because she often wore tight tops or ones that showed a lot of cleavage and he couldn't help but look at the snug top she wore now.

He tried not to look at her boobs. "Then why did you wear that today?"

She turned her head toward him and gave him a shy smile. "Because I was going to be with you."

His mouth opened but he couldn't form any words. She slipped her arm through his, pulled herself a little closer and rested her head on his shoulder. He soaked it all in as he tilted his head a bit to make contact with hers. When he did she squeezed his arm a little tighter and murmured. He couldn't believe it. *This-is-not-happening*.

They sat like that for several minutes without talking. When she moved her head he thought she wanted to sit up but she just looked into his eyes and her lips parted slightly. He didn't hesitate. He brought his mouth down to hers until their lips touched. Her free hand found his and their fingers locked together as she squeezed them tightly. Remembering how Cassie did it, his tongue found hers. They kissed for several minutes; he could see her erect nipples out of the corner of his eye when he opened them for a second. His cock felt like it was going to explode. When they broke their embrace they were both out of breath.

Maddie stood and held out her hand. "We should go back in."

He stood and they walked hand in hand to the door. She let go when he opened and they walked in as nonchalantly as they could. The clock on the wall told them the event ended in two minutes so they found their jackets and prepared to leave.

"How are you getting home?" he asked.

"My mom's picking me up, she's probably waiting outside."

"I'll walk you out."

She put her hand on his forearm. "It'd be better if you didn't."

Words stuck in his throat. "Maybe...maybe we could go out some time."

"I'm not allowed to go on real dates until I'm sixteen." She smiled at him. "But that's only three months away; we'll figure something out in the meantime."

He watched her as she walked toward the door. Before she reached it she stopped, paused, and turned around and walked back toward him. When she reached him her hand touched his forearm, she stood on tiptoes and kissed him on the cheek.

"Thank you for being such a gentleman – I just knew you would be."

# Chapter Twenty-One

The flow of blood slowed to a trickle by Saturday morning and Cassie felt like herself again. She was actually somewhat excited about her date as she got ready for it that afternoon. The more she thought about it the more she realized that Derek wasn't such a bad guy at all, in fact he was kind of cute. A lot of girls certainly thought so yet he asked *her* to go out. It felt good to be liked that way. He certainly didn't ask her because she had a reputation of being "easy," if anything it was just the opposite.

She'd been on a number of dates before but rarely more than once with the same guy. Most ended the same way, they would park somewhere or find a secluded spot if they had no car, and make out. She liked that. But invariably the guys wanted more. While kissing her a guy sometimes felt her boobs through her shirt. That didn't bother her because she wasn't that big and always wore a bra. What did bother her was when they would slip their hand under her shirt to try and feel her up. If they tried it once she just shoved their hand away. If they tried again that was the end of the date. That gave her a reputation as someone who didn't put out and she was okay with that. Better that than to be known as a "hand job honey" or "blow job queen," like some girls were. Though she pretended otherwise with her friends, she didn't even understand what a blowjob was except that you did it with your mouth.

Now that her period was ending Cassie started to feel horny again. Her mind wandered to Jake and she wanted to feel him on top of her, she wanted to feel him shooting his hot juice on her back. She wanted to see his cock, she wanted to touch it. She realized one more thing, because of her horniness if Derek tried to feel her up she was going to let him.

Cassie's mind wandered back to Jake. She hadn't talked to him since his mini-date with that girl Maddie. She did realize she'd been a bit unfair in the way she talked about her. A lot of girls didn't seem to like Maddie simply because she was so well assembled and that wasn't right, it wasn't her fault. If Jake liked her then she must be okay. Cassie did recognize and admit to the little bit of jealousy she felt the other day. At first she attributed to a period-induced hormonal swing, but she knew now that wasn't the case. It wasn't boob envy either. She was jealous of Jake liking Maddie more than her even though she knew that that was totally irrational and quite likely not the case.

She showered, did her hair and put on her makeup. Wearing her robe, she crossed from the bathroom to her bedroom. She noticed Jake was home so she made sure her door was closed so he wouldn't get the wrong idea. She tossed her clothes on the bed and started to get dressed. She wore her new jeans and was about to put on the sweater Jake gave her but thought better of it. If she was going to let Derek feel her up she didn't want it to be in that sweater. She selected a different, but also loose-fitting, sweater from her closet. She checked herself in the mirror, then checked the time – ten minutes to spare. She headed out to the living room.

Jake looked at her. "Wow, you look nice."

"Thank you. I have a date tonight."

"A date? With who?"

"Yes, a date...like you had yesterday. Derek is taking me to the movies."

"Derek? Oh."

Just then a car pulled up out front, he was right on time. She went out to meet him. She looked at the expression on Jake's face as she said goodbye. He looked crestfallen. He couldn't have expected to play since their mom was at the grocery store and would be back at any moment. She quickly realized he was jealous. *Like I was the other day.*


Derek discussed their movie options and told her to pick whatever she liked. He seemed ecstatic when she chose *Goodfellas* over *Edward Scissorhands*. They arrived at the theater with time to spare. He purchased a drink for each of them and bucket of popcorn to share. She was amused by how nervous he seemed though she was also surprised by how calm she felt, none of her typical first date anxiety. They settled into the seats just before the trailers began.

"You have another choice after the movie," he said.

"Which is?"

"Well, we could go to the diner as planned..."

"Or?"

"Friends of mine are having a little party tonight. They'll be food there."

"And drugs and booze, I suppose?"

"Definitely no drugs, my friends don't do that. There may be a little beer."

"I'll think about it."

The trailers started which gave her a chance to think. The party might be fun but it's not what she told her mom she was doing. Still, she was seventeen now and should be able to make her own decisions. She decided to see how she felt after the movie. Her thoughts turned from the party possibility to Jake. Unforeseen consequences from their activities were bound to happen though she just didn't expect jealousy to be one of them. It was definitely time for a serious talk.

Throughout the movie Derek held her hand for a bit and tentatively put his arm around her. His clumsiness amused her and she began to like him a bit more. When the movie ended she could tell he wanted to know her decision but seemed afraid to ask. She let him sweat just a little until they reached the parking lot.

"I have to be home by midnight at the absolute latest."

"We'll leave anytime you want."

They got to his friends house in only a few minutes. She calculated that it was only about ten minutes from her house which was good; she could walk it if she had to. She did lie about her curfew, it was actually twelve-thirty but she wanted to give herself a cushion. Fortunately he wasn't lying about the food, there were several boxes of pizza some of which were still warm. She helped herself to a slice while Derek introduced her to his friends.

"Can I get you a drink? Soda, water?" he asked.

"I thought you said there was beer."

Derek seemed surprised but he was quick to get her a can of Bud. Cassie didn't really drink but she figured one couldn't hurt. She'd tried hard liquor and didn't care for it at all, wine was okay but she liked the taste of beer. It went well with her pizza and she finished it fairly quickly. When she emptied her can Derek gave her another that she didn't really want. She checked the time and saw they had only about an hour left, not enough time to get drunk so she thought it was safe to have another. Halfway through the second one she felt it a little in that she became very relaxed. At quarter after eleven she told Derek they should think about leaving soon. She liked that he didn't hesitate and was quick to say goodbye and they left.

He politely opened the car door for her and they drove off. He realized he was heading straight for her house and wondered if he was in a hurry to get rid of her. He seemed to be having a good time, as was she. She hoped he was just concerned about getting her home without getting her in trouble for missing curfew. Normally she wouldn't say anything but she drank just enough to give her courage.

"You know we have some time yet."

He looked at her. "You want to..."

Cassie flashed a sheepish grin. "We can park and...*talk* for a bit."

Fortunately he got the hint without her having to spell it out for him. He found a place on a secluded side street under a canopy of trees. He turned the car off and looked at her. She looked at him but he didn't make a move so she reached for his head and pulled him to her until their lips met. He wasn't very good at making out. Not like Jake. Eventually he started getting the hang of it and they got into a groove. The alcohol loosened her inhibitions and heightened her horniness.

When he didn't make a move she took his hand and placed it against her boobs. He started to rub them, a little rougher than she liked but it was okay. He didn't attempt to go any further. She'd been thinking about it all day and she was determined to get felt up so she took one of his hands from her boobs and guided it under her sweater. He moved his hand up and felt her through her bra. This wasn't enough for her so she stopped, leaned forward and unfastened her bra. His hands now roamed freely over her boobs. She heard a load gasp and realized it came from her. Emboldened by her cry, he lifted her sweater up to expose her breasts. This wasn't in her plan but she wasn't about to stop him. His mouth found her right nipple and started sucking. She wasn't prepared for how good that felt.

"Oh god!"

She thrashed a bit causing her hand to land on his lap and she felt his hard cock without meaning to. He shifted to her left breast and sucked while his hand fumbled with the button of her jeans. This brought her to her senses and her hand locked around his wrist to prevent him from getting her pants open. He stopped but he was panting and she felt responsible. Without thinking she pushed him back in the seat and her hands went to his jeans and undid the buttons. She lowered the zipper and he lifted himself of the seat and lowered his pants enough to expose his cock. It was smaller than Jake's but every bit as hard. She wrapped her fingers around it and tugged on it the way Jake did and Derek exploded almost immediately.

Derek caught his breath and she realized he was covered with semen and it was all over his mother's car. Cassie found a tissue and did the best she could to help him clean up. He pulled his pants up as Cassie refastened her bra and straightened out her sweater.

"That...that was fun," Derek said.

"I'm glad you liked it.

He turned to her with a look of concern. "Please don't tell anyone I came so fast."

She smiled at him. "I won't as long as you don't say we did it at all."

# Chapter Twenty-Two

The exhilaration from his date stayed with Jake throughout the day Saturday. He still couldn't wrap his head around the fact that she invited him and that she initiated their make-out session. The quick lesson from Cassie certainly helped. He also realized that Maddie had some experience with this and that her holding his hand the way she did served as an impediment, an intentional one for sure, to him even attempting to fondle her boobs, not that he would have. His mom always drilled into him the importance of being respectful of other people, especially women, and it paid off here. He couldn't wait to see her again.

His euphoria dissipated when Cassie told him she was going on a date. She went on them before but not since they started with their games. He didn't understand why she didn't tell him until she was leaving. He also didn't understand why she was going with Derek, he didn't realize she liked the jock type. He contemplated starting to work out if that's what she wanted. The idea of what she might be doing tortured him, especially when she didn't come home until after midnight. He was awake in bed when he heard her come in. Consciously he knew she had every right to date and he certainly had no reason to expect that she wouldn't. As irrational as he understood his feelings to be, it still ate at him.

His mom made breakfast as she always did on Sunday morning. He did his best to act upbeat at the breakfast table but knew full well he wasn't doing a good job of it. Cassie was still in her room when he first sat down but she stirred shortly after and he saw her cross into the bathroom. A few minutes later she made her way to the table just as the pancakes arrived. As Cassie sat down their mom slid a plate of flapjacks in front of her. Cassie looked at him started to smile but stopped when she saw his expression. Their mom sat down with her plate and they all dug into their breakfast.

"How was your date?" their mother asked her.

"It was fun. We saw *Goodfellas*."

"I'd like to see that Edward Scissorhands, it looks good," their mom said. "I like Johnny Depp."

"That looks stupid," Jake said. "A guy with scissors for hands?"

"Well, grumpy speaks," their mom said.

"I'm not grumpy, just tired."

"What else did you do dear?"

Cassie glanced at Jake then turned toward her mother. "Not much, just grabbed a bite to eat. It *was* a long movie."

*Yeah right, I'll bet you did more than eat.* Jake finished his breakfast and put his plate in the sink without a word. He moped around the house alternating between his room and the living room the rest of the morning. At one point when their mom was out of earshot Cassie came over to him. She placed her hand on his shoulder and leaned into his ear and whispered, "We have to talk."

Cassie left the room and he retreated to his bedroom. He knew full well what came next. She would tell him they had to stop fooling around since she had a boyfriend. He knew that would happen at some point, he just didn't expect it to be so soon. He tried to console himself by saying they had a lot of fun and that he learned a lot in a short time. He also got to know his sister in ways he never expected and told himself he should be grateful. Unfortunately no matter what he thought it didn't help.

An hour or so later his mom came in to tell him she was leaving for a bit and would be back before dinner. She almost never went out on a Sunday except for an occasional errand and if she did she didn't announce her departure and expected arrival home. *Weird.* A few minutes later Cassie walked in and sat on the edge of his bed.

# Chapter Twenty-Three

When Cassie arrived home from her date her mom and Jake were both in bed. She knew her mom wouldn't be asleep and suspected Jake wasn't either. As she walked in the image of Jake's expression returned. She hoped he moved past the surprise and she regretted not having said something until just before she was leaving. She came in as quietly as she could and got ready for bed. She did her best to put Jake out of her mind for the moment. She thought of the way it felt when Derek sucked on her nipples and slipped her hand inside of her panties but it was no use and she gave up after a few minutes. She eventually drifted off to sleep.

The next morning she awoke in a very upbeat mood but Jake put a bit of a damper on that pretty quickly at breakfast. After he went to his room her mom asked her if she knew what the problem was and she lied and told her "no."

"He'll be sixteen in a few weeks," her mom said. "I hope he's not turning into a surly teenager."

"I wouldn't worry about that."

"He had that party at school Friday...he was going with some girl..."

"Maddie"

"That's her name. Maybe that didn't go so well."

"It probably went just fine mom."

"Could you talk to him? I tried but he says nothing's wrong."

"I'll talk to him."

She was relieved when her mother told her she would go out for a while so she could be alone with her brother. There was no way she could have talked to him with her mother around. After her mom left she walked into Jake's room and sat down on the bed, looked at him and waited for a response. He looked at her and looked away without a word.

"Care to tell me what bug's up your ass today?"

"I'm fine," he said.

"Bullshit. That's why mom was so concerned that she asked me to talk to you and left so I could."

"I'm okay, don't worry about me."

She shook her head. "Can you please stop being such an asshole so we can talk about this? We both know what this is about."

He looked at her but said nothing.

"Look," she continued, "I'm seventeen and I'm going to date, you're going to date too – you already have."

He finally spoke. "I know but..."

"I understand you feel a little jealous. Guess what? When you told me about Maddie I was jealous too."

"You were?"

"Yes I was. And I'll have you know my going on a date was your fault. You were making me so fucking horny I went out with Derek to get my mind off it."

He started to laugh and finally started to lighten up. "I...I was afraid you wouldn't want to do anything with me anymore because you have a boyfriend."

"Derek is not my boyfriend, we went on a date. We might even go on another but that still doesn't make him my boyfriend."

"But when you..."

"Stop," she said. "We have a lot to talk about before mom gets home but first I need to do something."

"What?"

"Pull your pants down...go ahead, pull them down."

He hesitated but finally did as she asked. She gently pushed him so he sat back down on the bed. He wasn't even hard as he sat there with his pants around his ankles. She scooted over until she was within reach and wrapped her hand around his cock. He instantly grew erect. She rubbed slowly up and down doing what she'd wanted to for a while now. She was enjoying herself, something she couldn't with Derek the night before because he came so quickly. She tried to do it the way Jake did it to himself. She slid her fingers up the shaft and over the head and back, she squeezed so the skin moved up and down with her motions, pausing occasionally to make him last longer. As he started breathing heavier and squirming a bit she went faster. His legs quivered and he shot a semen stream into the air and kept cumming as she stroked. She didn't stop until he was empty and her hand was covered with his goo. Then she did something else she was curious about – she licked a glob of it off of her hand to taste it.

She smiled at him as she licked her lips. "How was that?"

"Awesome, I didn't think you would ever do that."

"Good. If I'm dating I might want to do that to a guy but I want to be sure I'm good at it."

"Oh, you're good at it."

"Well I think I need more practice....a *lot* more practice. That is if you don't mind."

"Fuck no!"

She grinned at him and licked another glob of semen off the back of her hand. "Mmmm, tasty."

# Chapter Twenty-Four

Monday started off as a great day for Jake. He realized what an idiot he'd been the day before. *Time to grow up*. The new ground rules he and Cassie established made perfect sense. The best part was that she had absolutely no desire to discontinue their activities and he could stop worrying about it. She also teased him by saying she had something special planned for his birthday. He knew better than to try and get her to tell him what she had in mind so he would just spend the next few weeks driving himself nuts – exactly what she wanted.

At lunch that day Tony and Karl gave him a good ribbing about his date with Maddie. He let them have their fun and he actually enjoyed the attention, it almost gave him a celebrity status. He did suffer a bit of anxiety regarding Maddie and wondered if she meant it when she said she was interested in him. Those fears were quickly laid to rest after he spoke to her that morning. When he first saw her in class his mouth was once again too dry to speak, but then she smiled at him.

"I had a great time," he told her.

"Me too."

The major problem they faced was finding time to be together. They only had the one class in common and ate lunch at different times. The school was fairly large and they rarely crossed paths nor did Jake bump into Cassie very much. Maddie came up with their only solution for the moment.

"I do stuff after school a lot," she said. "If you can stay sometimes we can hang out a little then. I don't always have to go to my clubs. Are you able to stay at all?"

"Any day but Wednesday," he said.

She grinned shyly. "How about Thursday?"

"Just say where and I'll be there."

"I'll let you know Thursday morning." Her hand reached for his and squeezed. "You're a real good kisser and I'm glad you didn't...you didn't try to...try to feel me."

"I wouldn't do that."

Jake walked her partway to her next class and was almost late for his as a result. He couldn't get his mind off of her and his hard-on stayed with him all day. At one point he decided to go to the men's room and do something he hadn't in a very long time – jerk off into the urinal. That idea died when he walked in to find half a dozen guys hanging out in there. It would have to wait until he got home.

# Chapter Twenty-Five

Cassie waited for Teri in the cafeteria on Monday. The crisis with Jake resolved itself to the satisfaction of both of them. Their play would continue but at a reduced pace. He freely admitted he'd been passing up opportunities to be with his friends in order to be home every afternoon in case an opportunity to play with her presented itself. Instead they would make every Wednesday afternoon their play time since that was the day their mom worked late. She did tell him there would be no play during her monthly moon time. She also reserved to right to give him random hand jobs as she saw fit, not surprisingly he had no problem with that.

When Teri walked in Cassie did a double-take. Though it had only been a couple of weeks the weight loss showed in her face and she seemed a bit less "jiggley" when she walked. She also exhibited a bit of a swagger and seemed to hold her head up higher. It's not so much the weight she lost, probably not much more than ten pounds, but the attitude in the way she carried herself. Teri's major concern, her boobs, seemed bigger rather than smaller, probably because her belly didn't protrude as much. Cassie felt so proud of her friend.

"So tell me," Teri said, "how did the date go?"

"Oh the usual. We went to a movie, a party at his friend's house, made out a little."

Cassie filled in a few of the details as Teri asked questions but kept quiet about the sexual activity. She wanted to keep that private at least for now. She also told her about Jake and their new arrangement. Her friend updated her on the play with her brother.

"You know, we're not the only ones," Teri said.

"What do you mean?"

"You know Brenda from science? She kind of hinted that she lets her brother play with her boobs."

"Interesting, I guess plenty of people do it.

Teri changed the subject a bit. "You ever watch a porno?"

"No"

"Brian got a hold of one and gave it to me. It drove me crazy all weekend because I couldn't watch it since the VCR is in the living room. I stayed up late last night and watched it with the sound off after everyone went to bed. Oh –My – God! You wouldn't believe what these people do!"

"Weird?"

Teri shook her head. "No, fucking hot! You know what a blow job is, right?"

"Of course," Cassie lied.

"Well I didn't. There's no blowing involved – it's a lot of licking and sucking and taking the dick all the way in your mouth.

"Like eating an ice cream cone," Cassie guessed.

"More like a lollipop," Teri said. "The guys in the movie were huge but the girls had no problem. Brian says the films only use guys with really big ones and most guys aren't that big. You said Jake is big, right?"

"Bigger than Derek, that's for sure." Cassie immediately realized she'd slipped.

"You saw Derek's? You little bitch! I want details – now!"

Left with little choice, Cassie filled her in on the missing details. She also told Teri she wanted to borrow the tape if she could. Her friend agreed to bring it by that afternoon but she had to have it back as soon as possible because Brian had to return it to the friend he got it from.

"Will Jake be home?"

"Maybe, I'm not sure. Why?"

The rest of the day Cassie laughed at Teri's response whenever she thought of it. Her friend was becoming quite a character lately. The strange thing was that she wasn't sure if she was joking or not. Either way it was funny. Teri showed up at the house about four that afternoon and slipped her the tape. She wanted to watch it but didn't know if she wanted to see it while Jake was there; it might give him ideas for doings things she didn't want. She would decide whether or not to show him after she viewed it.

"Is Jake home?" Teri asked.

"He's in his room."

"Naked?"

Cassie laughed. "I doubt it."

"Too bad. Can I say hi?"

Cassie tapped on Jake's door and asked if he was decent. When he said he was she opened the door and they both walked in. She noticed the puzzled expression on Jake's face followed by the flash of recognition.

"Oh hi Teri, I didn't recognize you for a second."

Jake scooted over on the bed so they could sit down. They chatted a bit and Jake asked how Brian was doing. Cassie noticed Jake eyeballing Teri's boobs and felt another pang of jealousy. *I guess I do have boob envy.* She also noticed Teri eyeing Jake's crotch and she thought about what she said to her earlier. *Why not?*

"Jake, could you stand up for a second?"

Though a bit puzzled, he'd gotten used to following her instructions so he stood up. She slid around the bed until she sat directly in front of him. Her hands reached for the button of his jeans and she knew he realized what she was doing because she could see his cock growing and beginning to bulge in his pants. She slowly lowered the zipper, hooked her thumbs in the top of his jeans and underwear and tugged them down to his knees. His member stood at rapt attention.

"My god he's *huge!*" Teri yelped.

Jake beamed with pride. Cassie didn't touch his cock, she just let him stand there as Teri admired him, her mouth agape. Not wanting this to go any further, she pulled his pants back up, raised the zipper and buttoned his jeans. Obviously disappointed, Jake sat back down on the bed, his erection still clearly visible as it strained against the confines of his jeans. After a few minutes Teri said she had to get going and stood up. Cassie was starting to get up when Teri stopped at the doorway and turned back toward them.

"Oh Jake?" In one motion she lifted her shirt and bra up letting her boobs fall free. "It's only fair that you see me. I hope you like them."

Jake gasped. "Wow"

Cassie was impressed. For a heavier girl her friend's breasts seemed very firm even though they were so large, and her nipples were perfect. *Who wouldn't have boob envy?* Teri stood there for a moment and then put herself back together. She said goodbye and Cassie escorted her to the door. As she closed the door she started to laugh hysterically. *He probably came in his pants.*

"It's not funny," Jake called out from his bedroom.

She laughed even harder as she walked to his room. She thought about jerking him off but their mom would be home any minute. She stood at his bedroom door at looked in. He tried hard to look serious but couldn't help laughing himself.

"She was pretty impressed with you."

"She's pretty impressive herself."

"You should ask her out sometime, she'd probably let you play with them."

"I'll stick to Maddie for now."

She had to know. "Did you cum in your pants?"

"Almost. I almost came when you pulled my pants down, would have if you touched me."

He looked at her and she knew exactly what he wanted but there was no time. But she did want to take care of him. She walked across the hall and into the bathroom and stood next to the sink.

"Come in here."

He was at the door a few seconds later.

"Stand in front of the sink."

He moved over and faced the mirror. She stood to his right and placed her left hand on his shoulder. Her right hand unzipped him, unfastened his jeans and pulled his cock out. He braced himself by placing his hands on the vanity top as she started jerking his hard-on. It only took a few strokes.

*Arrggh!*

As he ejaculated she heard a car pull in the driveway. She tugged on him a few more times to get the last few drops out. Most of his semen landed in the sink but some hit the faucet and the initial stream covered the mirror.

"Clean this up really good." She swiped a glob of goo onto her finger and stuck it in her mouth as she left the room closing the door behind her.

# Chapter Twenty-Six

Like Teri, access to the VCR was a problem for Cassie. Taking a cue from her friend she waited until her mom and Jake were sound asleep. Though it was well past her bedtime and she needed to go to sleep, her curiosity compelled her to at least view some of the tape. She inserted it as quietly as possible and turned off the sound. She shifted the TV a little so it wouldn't be visible if her mom walked in the room. She fast-forwarded through the opening credits to the beginning of the film hoping the action started quickly. She did not have to wait.

The picture started with a naked woman working on a huge cock with her mouth and tongue. The scene mesmerized her and Cassie felt herself get extremely wet. She watched as the girl took the cock from her mouth and started pumping by hand as he shot all over her face until she was dripping with cum. The picture cut to another scene of a girl on her back thrashing about. A guy's face was buried between her legs and the camera zoomed in to show him licking her pussy. The picture cut again to show a man inserting his huge penis into a different girl's vagina and pumping away. She felt tingly and light-headed like she was about to have an orgasm. Without being aware of doing it she'd put her hand in her panties to finger herself. She grabbed a throw pillow and brought it to her face and bit into it just as her body shuddered and convulsed. She sat up, caught her breath and clicked off the TV. A minute later she realized she was nodding off so she got up and went to bed. *That was fucking unreal!*

The next morning Cassie awoke with a start. *Holy shit ! Holy fucking shit!* She realized she'd overslept, not only that she'd left the tape in the VCR. She vaguely recalled a tap on the door, her mother's knock to wake her up. She responded but fell back asleep. She quickly calculated how much time she had; if she hurried she could get to school just before class. She threw on some clothes and went into the bathroom to fix herself up as best she could though there would be no shower. She grabbed her shoes and went to the living room to retrieve the tape from the VCR. It was gone. *Fuck, fuck, fuck.*

She hoped that Jake somehow found the tape and took it though that dream shattered when she saw the note waiting for her on the kitchen table.

> *Cassandra,*
> *I'll be home early.*
> *We need to talk.*
> *- Mom*

*Oh fuck me!* Her heart pounded as she half-walked, half-ran to school. She slid into her seat just as class started but her mind roamed elsewhere. She mulled over what she could say to explain the tape. Nothing seemed plausible so she decided on an edited version of the truth. A friend loaned her the tape and she only watched it because she was curious. Then she would throw herself on the mercy of the court and hope for the best.

She left school immediately after her last class rather than hang for a while like she usually did. She didn't make any stops along the way and hoped Jake got home early as well. She wanted to explain what happened with the tape and see if he had a better idea for explaining it. As she reached sight of the house and saw her mom's car already in the driveway a chill traveled up her spine. A sense of dread surrounded her as slowly trudged those last few yards. *So this is how it feels to walk to the gallows.*

She walked in the door and there it was standing vertically on the table. She ignored it and went to her room and dropped her coat and books before going back to the kitchen to face her executioner. She stood there waiting, her legs trembling a little. A moment later her mom walked in.

"Oh good Cassandra, you're home before Jacob."

Cassie's heart raced and beads of perspiration formed on her forehead as her throat went dry. She would hear her mother out before she said anything to explain herself.

"I turned the TV on this morning to watch the

news but it was set to VCR mode. I got the shock of my life when I pressed play." She picked the tape up off the table. "I found this."

Her mother handed her the tape and she looked at the label – *Debbie Does It Again* – and realized her hands were shaking. Her mom took the tape from her hand and set it on the table and sat down. Cassie stood for a moment before sitting down as well.

"I don't know what to say to your brother. I don't know how to deal with this sort of stuff."

Cassie wasn't sure she heard her right. Then she realized her mom thought it was Jake's tape.

"Mom..."

"I know he...he pleasures himself. I see the evidence."

"Mom, he's not a little kid anymore."

"I know that, it's just so hard dealing with boys."

The reprieve from the governor elated her. After talking a little more she left the kitchen feeling as if a weight had been lifted off of her shoulders. By the time she reached her room another thought hit her and she marched back to the kitchen and stood over her mom.

"It's mine."

He mother looked up at her. "What?"

"The tape is mine, not Jake's. He had nothing to do with it."

Her mother's shoulders sagged as she let out a loud sigh. "I am so relieved."

She wasn't sure she heard right. "What?"

Her mother paused a moment before speaking again. "I guess you've seen it then."

"Very little, only a few minutes."

"Then you at least have an idea of what it's like. I don't want Jacob to get the idea that women are like that. It's so degrading."

"He doesn't think like that, mom."

"I hope not. So how did you get that, not from that boy out went with?"

"Derek? No, Teri found it and brought it over. I was just curious mom, that's all."

Her mom pushed the tape back toward her. "I understand. I was sixteen once."

"Seventeen"

"Seventeen," her mom shook her head. "I thought your brother was using it to...um."

"No mom, it was me."

Her mother chuckled. "At least when you do it you're not so messy."

Cassie felt her face flush. "Mom!"

Her mother smiled and laughed. "Well dear, you're not always so quiet. Don't be embarrassed, it's part of being a woman. Here's a news flash for you – I do it too sometimes."

The conversation had taken a totally unexpected turn and Cassie felt embarrassed and somewhat uncomfortable talking about masturbation with her mother. Her mom indicated that the tape had better disappear before Jake saw it, then she left the room and returned a minute later with a small box and handed it to her.

"I think you'll find this is a lot more fun. Don't worry, it's never been used. Try to be discrete since it makes a little noise."

# Chapter Twenty-Seven

Cassie saw Teri early in the day and told her to meet outside at lunch instead of the cafeteria. They could eat after they talked. She went to their usual spot and her friend was already there. She handed her the video tape and explained what happened.

"You're so lucky," Teri said. "My mom would have killed me."

"That's what I expected. Instead she gave me a vibrator."

"Did you try it? How was it?"

"Un-fucking-believable! You have to get one."

"What did you think about the tape? What you saw of it anyway."

"It gave me some ideas that's for sure," Cassie said.

"Did Jake see it?"

"I didn't have a chance to show him."

"You were right about his dick – he's fucking huge! Way bigger than Brian. Did you ever measure it?"

"Once. Jake said he was seven and a half but he's actually closer to seven and three-quarters."

"Brian told me he was seven but there's no way he's anywhere near that big, he's really thin too."

Teri looked at her watch and suggested they go inside to get some food. They went in and each grabbed a tray. Cassie took a slice of pizza but Teri stuck to her diet and selected a salad. The cafeteria wasn't crowded and they were able to get a table away from the others. Cassie ate her pizza quickly and realized how hungry she'd been since she'd skipped breakfast that day.

Cassie nodded toward the salad. "I see you're sticking to it."

"Down fourteen pounds and counting. At this rate I'll be ready for that beach by Fourth of July."

"The nude one?"

"Yup, I'm taking off every stitch and parading up and down all day. I want everyone to look at me."

"I couldn't do that, not in front of strangers

anyway. Why do you want to do that?"

Teri became animated. "Did you see the way Jake looked at me? That was the way Brian looked at me the first time. It's such a rush."

"I understand how you feel – sort of."

"Maybe I'll get a job at the *Tender Trap* when I'm eighteen."

"I must say that your boobs are impressive, but would you really want strangers pawing at you in a tittie bar?"

"That's just it, they can't touch only look."

Cassie shook her head. "That would be some first job on your résumé."

Teri laughed. "Brian's getting a job; he starts Saturday at the supermarket."

"That'll put a crimp in your...um...activities."

"Just the opposite, that's why he's getting it." Teri looked around to be sure no one could hear. "We're never alone, we need money for a motel room once in a while and...condoms."

Cassie's mouth dropped open. "You're going to *fuck him?*"

"Shhh, not so loud. Already have, a little bit anyway. I let him stick it in and take it right out. But I want to really do it. Don't you want to?"

"Yeah, I might sound corny but," Cassie said, "I know I'll always remember my first time and I want it to be with someone special."

"Jake's not special?"

"He is but he's my *brother*."

After lunch she went to class and the rest of the school day unfolded without incident. She thought of Teri going all the way with her brother and wondered what that would be like with Jake. Her plans for future activities included quite a few new things but she already determined that line will *never* be crossed. She smiled as she thought about what she had in mind for that afternoon and practically turned giddy when she thought about plans for his birthday.

# Chapter Twenty-Eight

Wednesday started off very strange for Jake. Cassie was still in her room which was unusual for her and his mother acted weird and hardly talked to him while he ate breakfast. Maybe it was his mom's time of the month; he assumed that at age forty-eight she still got her period. Whatever the issue he doubted it had anything to do with him. At school he only chatted briefly with Maddie in class but she did confirm their rendezvous for the following afternoon. The prospect of making out with her again kept his spirits sky high. Of course he took the usual ribbing from his buddies at lunch starting from the moment he walked in.

"Hey," Karl said. "Look who's here, If it isn't hot lips himself."

"Heard through the grapevine that the steps by the gym were smokin' on Friday," Tony said.

"You guys are just jealous."

Tony laughed. "Damn straight."

"I hear the hot lips run in the family," Karl said. "Rumor has it that your sister put a lip-lock on that football dude Derek."

"Jocks get all the babes," Tony said. "Tell your sister if she wants a real man she can call me."

Karl playfully shoved Tony and asked, "Why, so you can give her my number?"

"Fuck that," Tony said. "Cassie's fucking hot, why would she want a dweeb like you?"

Jake laughed along with them. "My sister has good taste, there's no way she'd go out with either of you two cretins."

They all laughed then focused on their lunch and the conversation shifted to other topics.

"We're heading to the mall after school," Karl said. "Or are you fondling Maddie's whoppers?"

"Not today," Jake said. "I have to head home."


The joking all happened in good fun but he felt good that his friends thought of Cassie as hot. He didn't mind that it was known that he made out with Maddie but it did trouble him that word got out around the school about his sister. He wasn't worried about her reputation because all kids made out on dates, some did so without going on dates. It just bothered him that people might think of Cassie as cheap. He thought of saying something to her but decided not to. He didn't want to upset her, especially today.

He arrived home a little after three. If Cassie came home in the next half hour or so they would safely have almost three hours of play time. She told him she had something different planned for today but of course she wouldn't give him the slightest hint. She also said she had something very special in mind to celebrate his birthday next week. As if that didn't drive him crazy enough, she bit her lip as she said it. He walked in the door and put his books down on the kitchen table and grabbed a can of soda out of the refrigerator. He drank half of it and carried the rest into the living room. As soon as he walked in he froze in his tracks.

Cassie stood in the living room, hands on hips and a stern look on her face as she glared at him. She wore only pink panties and bra.

"What the fuck are you doing? Why the hell aren't you undressed yet?"

He hesitated only a second before putting down the soda and scooting toward his room while pulling off his shirt.

"Move, move, move!"

He undressed in record time, his heart racing. He plopped down on the bed and looked at her. She pushed him backward, straddled him, grabbed his right wrist and tied something around it then fastened it to the headboard. She grabbed his left arm and did the same thing. She moved to his ankles and tied them so he lay spread-eagle on his back. His cock, of course, stood at full attention. She walked around the bed looking at him as he wondered what she had in store – he knew better than to ask. She touched the underside of his cock with her fingertips and pressed lightly. He almost exploded at her touch.

"Looks like your friend is ready to shoot. Unfortunately that won't be happening for quite some time. My mission for today is to drive you absolutely insane."

He strained to watch what she was doing. He felt her hand cup his balls, squeeze and tug. His cock bounced without being touched. This was going to be absolute torture and he was loving every minute of it.

# Chapter Twenty-Nine

Walking back and forth around the bed, Cassie admired her handiwork. The idea for the day's play dawned on her when Teri mentioned a scene from the video, one she never saw, that showed a woman tying up a man and whipping him. She had no desire to hurt Jake in any way but the idea of immobilizing him intrigued her. He'd gotten much better at holding back when he stroked himself and she was getting fairly good at sensing when he was about to ejaculate. Without telling him what she was doing, she tried controlling his orgasms when she stroked him. Though far from perfect, she picked up on the signs and could usually back off before it was too late.

One thing she noticed was that he shot much further when he was super excited. Her plan for today involved bringing him close without letting him cum and seeing how far she could make him shoot when she finally let him ejaculate. His testicles were the biggest telltale sign, when they got tight he was almost there. So every time they started moving closer to his body she planned to stop and wait until they relaxed and his cock wasn't as rock hard. He never seemed to go down all the way until after he ejaculated but he did get a little less firm. The real problem she knew was her because she loved watching him explode – she didn't know how long *she* could hold out. As she stood over him now she knew he could orgasm at the slightest touch so she needed to wait a while before putting her hand on him. *Let the teasing begin!*

She moved closer to the bed and turned away from him. "Like my ass?"

"Fucking love your ass."

She leaned forward and thrust it toward him as she pulled her panties up so they slid between her cheeks thong-like. "Tell me what you'd like to do to it."

She heard him sigh. "I want to kiss it, lick it, stick my dick between those gorgeous cheeks!"

She smiled and slowly backed toward him until

he kissed her ass but pulled away immediately after he did. As she turned back she looked at his cock and saw a drop of fluid on the tip as it throbbed. She thought he might even ejaculate without his cock being touched at all.

Cassie stood in front of him and struck a pose as she discretely unstuck the panties from her butt crack. She put her weight on one leg with a knee bent slightly, hips cocked, head turned partially to one side, and her tongue biting her lower lip – a moved she practiced in the mirror for a long time until she got it right. For a pièce de résistance she deliberately let a few wisps of her pubic hair protrude from her panties. He gasped as he looked her up and down before zeroing in on her crotch with a laser-focused stare. *Gotcha!*

She wiggled her hips just a little. "Tell me what you're thinking."

He gasped again. "I want to see your cu...I want to see your pussy."

She slowly shook her head. "Uh-uh-uh. You know the deal, my pussy is off limits."

"I just want to look."

Cassie had him right where she wanted him, going absolutely crazy and she hadn't even touched him yet. She moved in closer but out of reach and rotated her hips back and forth. His eyes never left her crotch. The panties she wore were perfect. They should be since she tried on almost every pair she had to see which were best. These were snug enough to accentuate her pubic mound and showed the faintest outline of her labia. She inserted her thumbs in the elastic and pulled as if she were going to lower them but stopped and backed away about a foot.

She cocked her head and bit her lip again. "Why do you want to see?"

"I just do, at least let me see your hair."

"Why?"

"Because...because your hair is blond yet your pubes are black."

"Mmm, they're more brownish. Why else do you want to see it?"

"Because I want to see if it's as sexy as the rest of you."

Cassie's eyes teared up. "You think I'm sexy?"

Jake's eyes widened. "Are fucking you kidding me? You know I do."

"You're so sweet."

"So can I see your pussy?"

"Hell no!"

She walked from one side of him to the other and stroked the inside of his thighs and intermittently fondled his balls. Cassie knew he would explode at the slightest touch so she waited for him to calm down a bit. After a while she stroked him a few times and stopped. She repeated this, along with more teasing, for the next hour until he was begging her to let him cum. She sat on the edge of the bed and watched the twitching of his blood-gorged muscle. Cassie looked toward him, his eyes pleading with her, his arms spread apart and raised slightly by the bindings fastened to the headboard. Jake's wrists were so loosely tied that a firm tug would set him free but she knew he wouldn't try since that would end the fun. She leaned forward and ran her fingertips over his scrotum and up the shaft of his penis until she felt the fluid oozing from the tip. He squirmed and let out a gasp as his cock jumped in anticipation when her fingers encircled him. His gaze locked on her as she slowly moved up and down and stopped again.

"Come on already, you're driving me fucking crazy."

She smiled. "I know – that's the idea."

His ass shifted as he tried to pull against her hand. "Damn it, finish me!"

She laughed and gripped him firmly for a moment while her free hand squeezed his balls and tugged down. His breathing quickened as she started stroking him. His legs quivered, his backed arched off the bed and he let out a loud grunt as a stream of semen forcefully shot out of his cock and landed on his chest with some reaching his shoulder. She kept pumping as he continued to ejaculate, a large, white pool forming on his stomach. The amount of fluid that he generated always astounded her and she never grew tired of watching him cum.

His head dropped back on his pillow, his eyes were closed and his arms relaxed. His breathing started returning to normal as his penis began to go flaccid. His eyes opened and looked at her as he tugged himself free of the bindings. She wiped her hand on his thigh to remove some of the goo that covered it. Her gaze followed the semen trail from his belly to his chest as her fingers wiped off the small glob that made it all the way to his left shoulder.

"Almost made it," she said. "A little more teasing and I'll get you to squirt yourself in the face yet."

"You're evil," he said.

"I know, and you love it."

"Damn straight."

She shook her head and grinned as she watched a rivulet of semen trickle down his side. She forgot to bring a towel with her so she started to get up and get one when a car door slammed and she heard footsteps coming up the walk.

"Shit, mom's home!"

"Fuck, she's early."

She ran to the hall linen closet, grabbed a towel, turned and tossed it to him. "Get cleaned up – I'll stall her."

# Chapter Thirty

Wednesday started off great for Jake and kept getting better, with best yet to come. He wore the shirt Cassie gave him the night before at his birthday celebration. Today was his actual birthday but his mom gave him the choice of celebrating a day before or a day after since she would be home fairly late on his actual birthday. He chose Tuesday because he didn't want to miss his time with Maddie. After what happened earlier that day he knew he'd made the correct choice.

The previous Thursday meeting with Maddie went well but was a bit strange. He noticed quite a few mixed messages which made him a bit unsure of where he really stood with her. She wore a button-down shirt which showed some cleavage and excited him. He suspected that she wore it intentionally though he couldn't be certain. They met in a semi-private area of the schoolyard near the athletic fields which allowed them to make out a bit. He was tempted to try to feel her boobs but he resisted the impulse. What he did do was look down her blouse as they kissed. Her orbs looked so soft and inviting that it was hard for him not to look. Unfortunately she realized what he was doing and fastened another button eliminating his view. He felt his face flushed when she caught him. He thought for sure he'd upset her but she seemed fine, though she did leave a short time later.

That night he convinced himself that he'd blown it with her but the next day she didn't act any differently than normal. Monday she'd mentioned she looked forward to Thursday and all was right in his world again. This morning she'd surprised him with a birthday card, she surprised him even more by saying she wanted to see him at lunchtime – his lunch – even though it meant she had to skip a class. She told him she needed to explain some things to him and felt his birthday was the right time to do it. They met at their usual spot on the athletic field, though it was fairly crowded at that time of day.

"You probably think I'm weird," Maddie said.

"Of course not, why do you say that?"

"Because I am weird sometimes. The other day when we were kissing..."

"Maddie, I'm sorry about that. I ..."

"Don't be, you were only doing what I *wanted* you to do. But when you did I got weird."

"You wanted me to..."

"Yes! While we were walking over here I opened two buttons without you noticing."

"But why...?"

"I'll try to explain but it's complicated. It involves my mom. She's, uh, big up top like me, it's where I get it from. It also involves my uncle, my dad's brother."

Jake tried to follow what she was saying. Okay, and...?"

"He was always my favorite uncle but when I started um...developing... he got a little too friendly. He would always be wrestling with me and grabbing me there and pretending he was kidding or that it was an accident. I complained to my mom but she thought I was overreacting. She said she went through that kind of stuff when she was my age and I should learn to deal with it."

"I take it there's more," Jake said.

Maddie shook her head. "I tried to deal with it but it kept getting worse. One day he wrestled with me and put his hand all the way up my shirt and slipped it inside my bra. I screamed really loud and my mom came running in and caught him before he could remove his hand."

"Holy shit!"

"It gets worse," she said. "My mom called the cops and had him arrested. My dad got mad at my mom for doing that and it was a long time before things got back to normal."

"Did he go to jail?"

"No but he got in big trouble. He had to go to counseling and he isn't allowed anywhere near me until I'm eighteen. Then it's up to me whether I see him or not. He did write me a letter apologizing."

"I'm sorry you had to go through that."

"I was only twelve at the time. My mom told me that because of how I'm built a lot of guys will pretend to like me when they only want to get their hands on my...um...boobs." Maddie blushed as she said it. "So I'm always thinking that's why a guy says he likes me – because he wants to touch them."

"That's not why I like you," Jake said.

"I *know*, that's why I've been weird. I'm always afraid someone will try to touch them...but I want *you* to."

"You *want* me to?"

"Yes!"

She looked around the schoolyard for a moment. Then she grabbed the back of his right hand, slowly brought him up to her chest and pressed it against her left breast. She held it there for a moment as he cupped her massive boob and gave her a very light squeeze. She pulled his hand away again.

"See, I knew you'd be gentle. We should be going."

As they walked away he was thinking that this was the most incredible birthday he ever had and the best was yet to come. He couldn't imagine what Cassie had in store for him though she hinted at it when she told him the shirt was a decoy and he would be getting his "real" present on his "real" birthday.

# Chapter Thirty-One

There would be no near-disaster this week – she wouldn't allow it. Cassie felt responsible for almost getting caught the week before. She didn't double check that her mom was indeed working late last Wednesday. As it turned out that the previous week someone had asked her mom to switch late days with her and she worked late on Thursday instead. Had she come home just five minutes earlier Jake would have been caught with his pants down, or off in this case, and her with her brother's dick in *her* hand. After tossing Jake a towel she barely had time to throw on her sweats and as she talked with her mom in the kitchen she realized that her hand was still covered with some of Jake's semen.

This week she confirmed that her mom would be late by calling her at work to discuss dinner and whether she would want something when she got home. That taken care of, she focused on getting ready. She skipped her last class of the day and came home early so she could shower, shave her legs, paint her nails and look her best. For the last couple of weeks she'd thought about what she could do to make the day special for him. She came up with a number of different scenarios that would take them further than they'd ever been. As she thought about it something dawned on her, it was *his* birthday. Everything she'd been thinking of was something that would excite *her*. After that epiphany she knew exactly what to do and she'd been practically giddy ever since.

Her preening complete, Cassie slipped on a robe and left the bathroom. He would be home any minute so she wrote a quick not and left it on the table where he would be sure to see it. Then she went to her room and waited. She heard him come in a few minutes later. He stopped in the kitchen briefly before she heard him go to his room. She waited a couple of minutes before leaving her room, walking across the hall and standing in his doorway.

# Chapter Thirty-Two

The steam in the house told Jake his sister was home and had been, or still was, in the shower. He saw the note on the table, read it and took it with him to his room. Following the directions, he removed his clothes, sat on the bed with his back against the headboard and waited. A moment later she stood in the doorway wearing her white terrycloth robe. Cassie walked around to the foot of the bed and faced him. She lowered her head while raising her eyes and biting her lower lip. She relaxed her shoulders allowing her robe to slide off and fall to the floor. Jake's jaw hung open as his sister stood there – *naked*.

He eyed her from head to toe. Her blond hair stopped just above her shoulders. Her blue eyes glistened, as did her glossed lips. Her small, perky and pert breasts with perfectly shaped nipples called to him.

His eyes travelled down past her tight stomach and "innie" navel until they reached her triangular patch of light brown pubic hair. He eyed a little mound and the lip-like labia of her vagina peaking through her perfectly sculpted bush. He noted the pale-white thighs, toned calves and even the painted toes of her feet. As his eyes traveled back up she slowly rotated 360 degrees so he could take in her naked ass. As she faced him once more he was speechless. She was even more perfect than he'd imagined.

"Happy birthday, Jake. I hope you like your present."

He tried several times before he could finally form the words. "I'm...I'm in absolute awe. You are beautiful, you are gorgeous...you are absolutely stunning."

Cassie blinked several times before she spoke with damp eyes and a cracked voice. "Thank you. Now let me tell you about your present."

"There's more? I thought seeing you naked *was* my present."

"No Jake, *I'm* your present. My body is yours.

You can do anything you like with it or ask me to do anything to you. The only thing you can't do is put your penis in my vagina, anything else goes – *anything*."

Jake couldn't believe what he heard and he didn't know where to begin so he just looked at her for a moment. He got up und stood in front of her. The back of his hand slowly skimmed the surface of her skin and over her nipples which perked up at the touch. His fingers found the bottom of her chin and gently titled it upward. She looked at him and closed her eyes as her lips parted. He bent down and put his lips to hers and their tongues found each other. He moved in close until their bodies touched. Being a head taller, his erection pressed into her stomach. A month ago he would have ejaculated at first contact, now it merely felt incredible as she pushed herself into him.

The kiss broken, his lips moved down the side of her neck as she tilted her head to allow him access. He moved across her chest and down to her right breast until he settled on the nipple and sucked gently. She shuddered as it became erect. *Ohhh!* He moved across to the other nipple and did the same. He felt her knee rubbing against his cock and knew he couldn't hold out for long. He backed his head a few inches away and closed his eyes in an effort to bring himself under control but it wasn't working. Instead he spun her around and bent his knees to lower his cock to her ass. He pulled her close so his penis nestled between her cheeks, wrapped his arms around her waist and pulled her in close. He started moving against her as she wiggled her ass into him.

*Arggghhhh!*

As he ejaculated his legs buckled and they both collapsed onto the bed with him on top of her. They lay there for several minutes as he regained his composure. He grabbed the towel he kept on the side of the bed and wiped his semen off of her back and his crotch. Cassie started to turn on her side but he nudged her gently so she would remain face down. He slid up on the bed until he could reach the back of her neck and nibble on it. He worked very slowly down her spine kissing, licking and tasting her. He reached the small of her back then kept moving to her soft cheeks, alternating between them. He moved on to her left thigh and worked his way down to her feet. She let out occasional murmurs and soft "oohs" as he started working up her right leg. He reached her ass cheeks again and licked between them and even tasted her anus.

He had her roll over on her back as he sat up and took a good look at her. He didn't take for granted that he would ever see her this way again so he wanted to take it all in and savor every moment. He again started nibbling at her neck and kissed his way to her breasts. He spent a lot of time sucking and licking her nipples as she squirmed and cooed. He worked his way down to her stomach and kissed and licked all around her bellybutton. He moved to her pubic region, and though he was anxious to explore it, he moved past and down her legs until he reached her toes. He kissed her feet and started working his way back up. He resisted the urge to hurry and it was several minutes before he rested his head on her hip with his gaze fixed on her vagina.

Jake slowly traced the border of her pubic hair with his fingertips. He was fully erect again but without an urge to ejaculate. He ran his fingers through her pubes and then lightly touched her labia. Cassie squirmed a bit more and gyrated her hips. He ran his finger down her lips and back up again before separating them. When he ran his fingers down them again he realized how wet she was. He brought his fingers to his mouth to taste her juices and was pleasantly surprised. His friends made jokes about how fishy and funky women smell but he thought Cassie tasted delicious. He moved closer so he could see every detail as his fingers roamed over her pussy. He inserted one finger inside of her vagina and she gasped sharply and arched her back. She was very tight and he wasn't sure how his penis would fit in there if she ever did allow him to try. After slowly moving his finger in an out he slid it out of her and back up the lips. He travelled up until he reached what looked like a little button under a hood of flesh. He eyed it for a moment before touching it.

*Arrrh! Oh god!*

Her reaction startled him but Jake realized he'd found her clit. He climbed over her legs and pushed them apart so he could settle in between them and lay on his stomach with his face at her bush. He wanted to try something he'd heard people talking about and hoped he didn't screw it up. He tentatively brought his mouth to her pussy and licked her lips. Cassie gasped and her legs seemed to shiver. He liked the reaction and he liked the way she tasted. He tried not to be too rough as he moved his tongue up and slowly licked her clit.

*Ahhh! Oh shit....oh fuck...oh god...yes, yes...oh fuck yes!*

# Chapter Thirty-Three

Blond hair twirled around as Cassie's head tossed from side to side on the pillow. Her fingers ran through Jakes hair as she palmed the back of his head to pull him close, push him away and pull her back in again. Sensations coursed through her body, jolts of electricity she'd never felt before. Her breath came in ragged gulps as perspiration moistened her skin. She gasped for air as she felt his tongue slowly work down her labia before he pushed it into her vagina. Just as she regained her senses he slipped his tongue out and started working back toward her clit. Her thighs quivered in anticipation. They shook uncontrollably when his tongue reached its destination. *Oh shit....oh god....arggghhhh!*

Her hands pushed his head away. "I...I can't....I can't take anymore."

Cassie nudged him and he slid up next to her and put his head on her chest. She gently stroked his hair as his finger traced the outline of her boobs. She had no idea she was capable of feeling so good. She thought the vibrator induced orgasms were intense but they weren't even close to what she'd just experienced. She glanced at the clock and saw they still had plenty of time, at least two hours though she would only allow half that so there would be no repeat of the previous week. That would be plenty of time for her to try something she'd been thinking about. She just hoped she didn't mess it up.

Rolling over on her side, Jake slipped off of her. She kissed him and tasted her juices on his lips and thought they weren't as unpleasant as she'd feared. She had him lay back and she put her head on his chest. Her fingers ran over his pecs and circled his nipples. Her eyes were on his cock as she watched him grow erect again. She slid down a little further so her hand could reach low enough to fondle his balls. She released his testicles and ran one finger up the underside of his cock. She lingered on the area where the skin changed and felt much softer. She circled the mushroom-like head and watched a drop of clear fluid ooze from the tip. She wiped it with her finger and brought it to her mouth where she licked it off. She watched another drop form and slid down so she could lick it off with her tongue. She licked the entire head and then moved her tongue down the shaft. She kept going until she could lick his balls and alternated between licking and sucking on them. She paused briefly to remove a pubic hair from her mouth, then licked the shaft again. Jake murmured with approval when she reached the head. She pulled back to look at his cock and felt nervous about what she was going to do.

She wrapped her hand around the base of his cock. "Tell me if I'm not doing this right."

She took the head in her mouth and realized how big he really was. She inhaled and slowly lowered herself onto him until she started to gag. She wrapped her fingers around his cock just above that point and knew she could go that far down without having to worry about gagging again. She came up even slower with her tongue pressing the underside of his cock. She came up off of him. Still holding him with one hand she used the other to move the hair out of her face while she worked up some moisture in her mouth. When she was ready she took a deep breath and went back down. She moved up and down while varying her speed and flicking parts of his cock with her tongue. She paid attention to his moans to get a sense of what he likes.

His fingers ran through her hair. "Oh man, that's...that's incredible."

She went a little faster and he started to moan louder. His legs started to tense up and her free hand felt his balls moving closer to his body. She saw his hand clench the bed sheet and his toes start to curl. His hand tried to push her head off of him but she resisted his effort.

"I'm gonna cum!"

She took him as far down as she could as she felt his cock pulsate as a hot stream hit the back of her throat. She pumped him with her hand and tried to swallow his semen as fast as it spewed out of him but she had to come up for air before the last few drops came out. After she caught her breath she put her mouth back on his rapidly deflating penis and licked it clean. Then she climbed up next to him and laid her head on his chest.

His fingers stroked her hair. "That was incredible."

"I'm glad you liked it." She looked up at him and smiled. "Happy birthday, Jake."

They stayed there in each other's arms for several minutes without saying a word. Cassie sensed Jake was falling asleep as she tried to soak in everything she was feeling, both physically and mentally. She was content but at the same time conflicted. After a few minutes she shifted a bit and felt him stir.

Her finger slowly ran over his flaccid penis. "Jake?"

"Hmmm?"

"You do know what we're doing is wrong?"

Jake paused before speaking. "I know, but I don't want to stop."

"Me neither."

# Chapter Thirty-Four

*June 2016*

Fingers twirled the white goo draining into his navel. Cassie licked her fingers and stood up while he caught his breath. She washed her hands in the bathroom and then went into the bedroom to strip off her clothes. She took a towel from the bathroom and a pillow from the bed and went back into the living room, tossed the pillow on the floor and the towel to Jake. He caught it in midair and wiped himself without taking his eyes off of her.

He tossed the towel aside. "You're still gorgeous. Working out again?"

"A little, I'm entering my prime cougar years so I have to stay toned."

"Well you look absolutely delicious as always."

Cassie smiled. "Good because you've got some eating to do."

Jake positioned the pillow in the middle of the floor while Cassie took two smaller throw pillows from the couch. He dropped to the floor and positioned himself with his head resting on the pillow and she tossed a smaller pillow on either side of him. When he was set she planted her feet so she straddled him and lowered herself so she squatted down hovering just over his chest. She repositioned the throw pillows and kneeled down on them. Then she leaned forward with the palms of her hands resting on the floor next to his head. Jake ran his hands over her breasts and gently pinched her erect nipples.

*Mmmm*

"Still nice and firm," he said.

"The advantage of small boobs, not like that girl you dated in high school."

"Maddie"

"That's the one. Oh yeah, that feels nice..."

Cassie moved up to straddle his face and lowered her body until she felt the tip of his tongue. She moved closer for a bit, pulled away, moved back in and pulled away once more. She loved this position because she was in total control, at least until she *lost* control. She felt his tongue work up and down her labia. When he reached her clit she inhaled sharply, lowered her head, closed her eyes and bit her lower lip. When she felt the intensity building she backed away for a moment so he would stop. This went on for almost twenty minutes until she no longer had the willpower to delay her orgasm so she lowered herself to his mouth and stayed there. She closed her eyes as her legs quivered and then shook in earnest. She gulped air as she placed her hands on the floor behind her and arched her back.

*Arrrrghhh......oh god...oh, fuck yeah!*

She sat on his chest but kept most of her weight on her knees. Her head stayed down and eyes closed as she regained her composure. She opened her eyes to see him grinning at her and she started to laugh.

"God, I needed that. Nobody eats me like you do."

"Happy to be of service," he said. "You know, most women have a series of little' orgasms and maybe a nice one to top it off. But you build to a monster 'O' like no one I ever met."

She bent down to kiss him. "It's that skilled tongue of yours. I'll tell you this – you're getting a killer blowjob when we go to bed."

"My tongue learned from your coaching."

"Bullshit, you have a natural talent," she said. "That was clear from the first time you did it and it had nothing to do with me. I was just the lucky recipient."

Jake picked the pillows up from the floor while Cassie went into the bedroom and returned with a comforter. She had him take his sweats off so their naked bodies could snuggle under the blanket. They each had another glass of wine while they reminisced a bit. Jake talked about the last time he saw Maddie. They'd stayed friends after they went their separate ways following high school. She talked about Teri and how they remained fairly close all these years though her friend had the life Cassie expected for herself. Teri was the typical suburban soccer mom ferrying three kids around to various activities. What really impressed Cassie was that Teri not only hit her weight loss goal, she'd kept it off all these years. She laughed when she thought about the day at the nude beach when Teri remained true to her word and paraded herself around naked while she and a lot of other people watched.

"What's so funny?" Jake asked.

"Just thinking about Teri, she was such a character back then."

"You know she was the first pair of boobs I ever saw. What ever happened with her dancing career? With a rack like that she should have made a fortune."

"It's funny now but back then it was a real fiasco. She got hired at the *Tender Trap*, as you know."

"I know. Me, Tony and Karl tried to see her dance once but we couldn't get in because we were still only seventeen. By the time we were old enough she wasn't there anymore."

"Teri made me swear I wouldn't tell anyone but I guess it's okay now. She was dancing there for only a week or so when it happened. A guy walked in and sat down at the bar. She just kept dancing and thought nothing of it."

"Let me guess – she knew the guy."

"I'll say, it was her dad."

"Holy shit. That must have been awkward."

"That doesn't begin to describe it. It gets much worse. When she got home her dad was waiting for her. When Teri asked him not to tell her mom he said he wouldn't on one condition – she let him play with her boobs."

Jake shook his head. "That's fucked up. Did she?"

"No. She told her mom herself and then told her what her dad wanted to do. Let's say the shit hit the fan. Her parents almost got divorced and she quit dancing. Now look at her."

"I wish we knew her secret," Jake said.

"You and me both."

"Did we fuck ourselves up? I mean what we did...what we still do is not normal for a brother and sister."

"Maybe, who knows? Though, it didn't seem to bother Teri."

Jake stared at her for a moment. "You mean they...Teri and Brian?"

"Unlike us they went all the way, fucked like rabbits for years and still do sometimes."

"Wow, I had no idea."

"They're not the only ones either," Cassie said. "I know of a few other girls that did some things with their brothers like us and most of them turned out okay."

Jake got up and went to the kitchen while she emptied the last of the wine into their glasses. He returned with some chips and dip and set in on the table. Cassie went to use the bathroom and returned a few minutes later. Jake settled back in under the blanket but she wandered around the living room a bit because she knew he liked looking at her naked body. She wanted to make him feel every bit as good as he made her feel and that started by getting him hot. After doing this for a few minutes she started getting chilly so she curled up next to her brother under the blanket. Her hand touched his crotch for a moment and felt his erection. *Mission accomplished.*

Jake put his arm around her. "If it's not because of our...activities, maybe I'm just too picky."

Cassie sat back. "What is your idea of the 'perfect' woman?"

"Wow, interesting question."

"Let me guess, big boobs!"

"Nah, Maddie got me over that one, after playing with those whoppers nothing else compares. Now I just want boobs that fit the woman's body and absolutely no fake titties for me."

"What else?"

He paused a moment. "I want a smart woman, one who has an opinion about things and can back it up with logic."

"What about looks?" she asked.

"She should be pretty of course and I want her to be shorter than me, though not too short. Petite with a killer ass would be nice."

Cassie pretended to be making a list. "Go on, what else?"

"She has to be comfortable with her own body and not be complaining about being fat or that some part isn't right. She also can't be stuck up and think she's beautiful either."

She added it to the pretend list. "Quite a paradox. Continue."

"She has to like being naked, especially around me. Oh, and this is a big one, no shaved pussy. I want a nicely manicured bush."

She mimicked turning the page on a pad. "Page two. Keep going."

"Personality is important. She has to be spontaneous and willing to take risks. A sense of humor is critical and she can't take life too seriously. On the other hand she needs to be level headed when she should be."

"Another paradox. Continue."

"She has to love sex and want a lot of it. I don't want a woman who does it because she's supposed to or because that's how you get a guy. I want her to care about pleasing me but I really want her to care about being sure her own needs are met. She also has to like all kinds of sex and be willing to experiment."

Cassie pretend scribbled some more. "Anything else?"

"Yeah," he said. "We need to have a very real and very deep connection. She needs to totally love me and I need to be head over heels in love with her."

Cassie flipped through the make believe pages. "That would be an impressive specimen. However, I'm sorry to say that such a woman does not exist."

"Sure she does."

"In your dreams maybe," Cassie laughed. "I'm sure you can find part of what you want but a woman completely like your ideal is not real."

"Sure she is."

Cassie looked at his serious expression. "How can you be so sure?"

"Because I just described you."

Cassie wasn't sure she'd heard him correctly. She was about to ask him to repeat it but his demeanor told her all she needed to know. She tried to speak but couldn't. Her lip started to tremble as her eyes welled up with tears cascading down her cheeks seconds later. She threw her arms around his neck and squeezed him tight. Their lips met and they kissed slowly and tenderly. She tossed the blanket aside and threw her leg over his so she straddled him. As they kissed her right hand reached down and found his hard cock. Then she did something she'd never done before – she guided him into her pussy.

She slid down until he was all the way inside her. She didn't move at first, she just wanted to feel him. He was larger than any guy she'd ever had and he filled her like no one before. She started gliding up and down very slowly. She broke their kiss and she moved her head to the side of his and started gasping for air. He rolled her on to her back without slipping out of her. He started thrusting very slowly as if he wanted to feel her as much as she did him. He began to vary the speed and depth of his thrusts, pausing occasionally. *My god he knows how to fuck....why didn't we do this before?*

Air came in gulps now as she felt it building inside of her. He was breathing heavier as well and she knew he was getting close. She felt light-headed and started feeling a way that normally only happened when using a vibrator or being eaten. A tingle of electricity surged through her just as he stiffened and let out a loud grunt.

*Oh shit....arrggghhh...oh shit....oh god!*

In his bed their bodies intertwined underneath the blanket. He lay on his back and ran his fingers through her hair. She didn't remember ever feeling so content. He moved a little bit but she didn't let go.

"That was so nice," she said.

"It was. Um, Cassie...I've been thinking."

"About what?"

"About us."

She sensed his nervousness and sat up to look at him. "What about us?"

Jake took a deep breath. "Please hear me out before you say anything."

Now *she* was nervous. "Go....go on."

"All those things I said, I hope you realize I meant them. That really is what I think of you. I haven't been able to find anyone because I've been looking for you. When I fantasize it's about you. You're the woman I want."

"Jake, I..."

"No please, hear me out. We could move somewhere where no one knows us. We don't look that much alike and we already have the same last name. I can easily get an engineering job in just about any city."

Cassie was confused. "What are you saying?"

"We can go somewhere and live like a married couple, get rings and everything. Cassie the woman I want to marry is *you*."

Cassie was stunned and it took her a moment to wrap her head around what he was saying. There was no doubt how much she loved him and no one had ever made her feel the way she did sexually. But this was out of left field and something she'd never remotely considered. She looked at his face as it displayed a combination of hope and fear.

She shook her head. "Jake, I love you. But you are a fucking asshole."

Jake looked like he was in shock. "I...I'm sorry. It was just an idea."

She looked at him and bit her lower lip. "Why the hell didn't you ask me ten years ago? Yes, I'll pretend marry you!"

"You...you will?"

"Yes! Now shut up and fuck my goddamn brains out!"

# About the Author

J.W. Richard is a freelance journalist and a graduate of the University of Nevada, Las Vegas. Originally from New York, J.W. currently resides in Las Vegas, Nevada.